D1273297

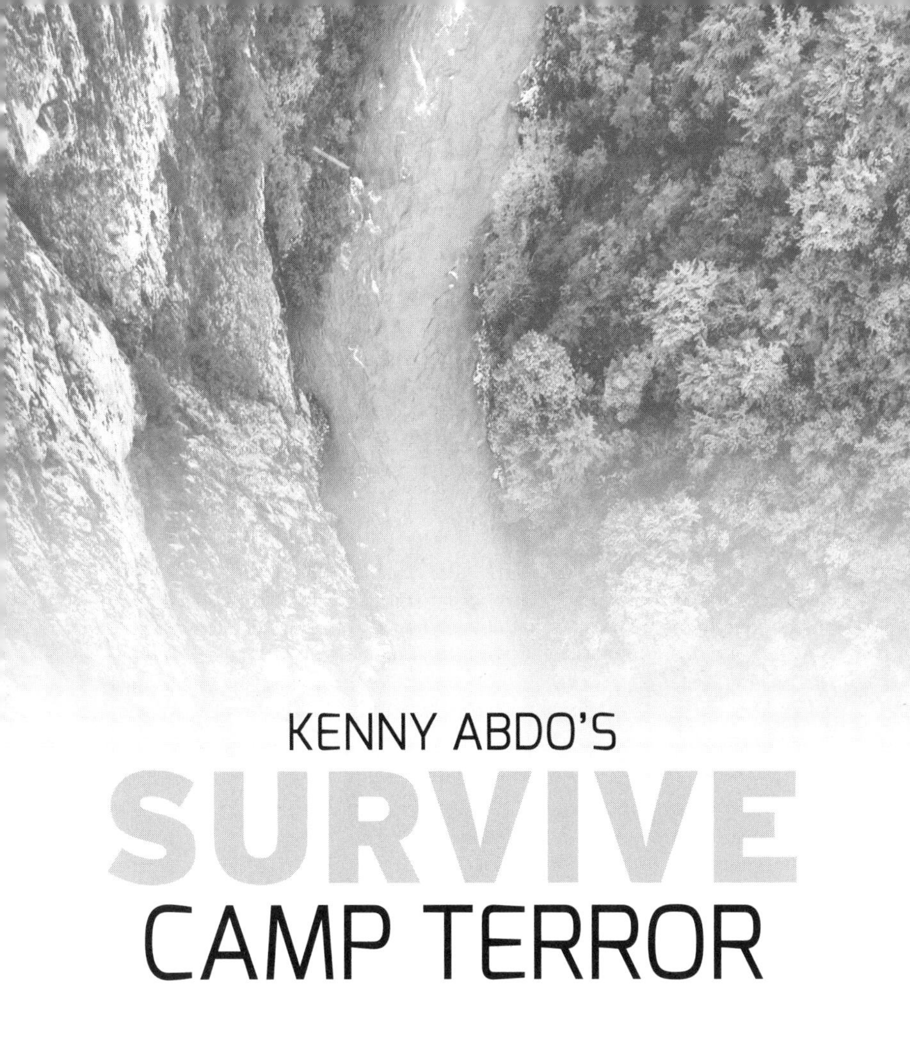

KENNY ABDO'S

SURVIVE
CAMP TERROR

EPIC
Escape
An Imprint of EPIC Press
EPICPRESS.COM

Camp Terror
Survive

Written by Kenny Abdo

Published by EPIC Press™
PO Box 398166
Minneapolis, MN 55439

Printed in the United States of America.

Cover design by Christina Doffing
Images for cover art obtained from iStockPhoto.com
Edited by Rue Moran

LIBRARY OF CONGRESS CATALOGING-IN-PUBLICATION DATA
Names: Abdo, Kenny, author.
Title: Camp Terror / by Kenny Abdo.
Description: Minneapolis, MN : EPIC Press, 2018. | Series: Survive
Summary: After decades of being closed, Camp Dream Haven has reopened to a new generation. When a rafting excursion ends in disaster, two campers, Maddy and TJ must survive in the wilderness. But as they forge their way back to camp, they suspect they are not alone.
Identifiers: LCCN 2016962620 | ISBN 9781680767292 (lib. bdg.) | ISBN 9781680767858 (ebook)
Subjects: LCSH: Camping—Fiction. | Disasters—Fiction. | Wilderness survival—Fiction. | Adventure and adventurers—Fiction. | Rafting (Sports)—Fiction. | Fear—Fiction. | Survival—Fiction. | Young adult fiction.
Classification: DDC [Fic]—dc23
LC record available at http://lccn.loc.gov/2016962620

EPICPRESS.COM

"Things do not change; we change."
—Henry David Thoreau, *Walden*

"I told the others, they didn't believe me.
You're doomed. You're all doomed."
—Crazy Ralph, *Friday the 13th Part II*

PROLOGUE

NO MATTER HOW FAST HE WAS RUNNING, Edgar Hugo could hear the steps behind him getting closer. Every branch he tripped over, every rock his foot stumbled on, Edgar got closer to the brink of being caught. The night was clear, allowing the moon to guide young Edgar through the woods as best as it could. If it weren't for his one dead eye, he would have been able to dodge the trees coming at him more easily. The night would have been just as quiet, too, if it weren't for Edgar's own heartbeat echoing in his ears.

Any time poor Edgar looked over his shoulder, the

Shape pursuing him grew larger. And the knife that the Shape carried, as long as Edgar's forearm, glowed in the moon's sinister light. Poor, helpless Edgar could feel the cold breath of his hunter on his already goose-bumped neck.

It was just going to be eight weeks, Edgar's parents promised. He would learn to live with his disability. They said that it was important to go out into the world—to not be scared of it. They said it was vital to grow as a person during the summer away from his safe place. His safe place being the basement, where he would dwell within his books of fantasy and horror.

Sitting in their kitchen nook, Edgar's parents were actively thinking of the best way for their ten-year-old to spend his summer. No longer did Dick, a quantum physics professor at the local community college, want to see his boy get beaten both mentally and physically because of what he could not control. No longer did Helen, junior editor of the hometown gazette, want her husband to fret over who their son would grow up to be. Together, what Dick and Helen Hugo really desired was what all parents wanted for their child: for him to be happy.

As Edgar finally stumbled into the Bastion, a fake wooden castle that the locals used for paintball matches deep within the woods, he felt a momentary sense of relief. Crouching behind a mountain of barrels labeled PAINTBALLS, the ten-year-old boy caught his breath, in and out, making it as silent as possible.

When he heard a twig snap in front of him, Edgar placed one hand over his own mouth, taking in air with his nostrils only when absolutely necessary. As the Shape moved toward the barrels, it made a disturbing laugh through its breath. Edgar had to think of something, and he had to do it fast. Picking up a rock buried below his muddied, Velcroed shoe, Edgar gave it a soft lob across the Bastion, diverting the Shape towards that direction.

With his brief moment, Edgar ran as fast as his young legs could in the opposite direction. He wanted to close his eye and believe he was in his basement, reading his *Fangoria* magazines and drinking Mountain Dew. He wanted to feel the sunshine on his face as he sat in the kitchen nook waiting for his breakfast. What he didn't want to feel was the root stuck deep within the earth taking his small body to the ground.

Unfortunately, what Dick and Helen Hugo hadn't realized, or anticipated, rather—while flipping through their pamphlet on Camp Dream Haven that spring of 1986, looking at all of the smiling children brandishing bows with arrows and jumping off of docks—was that Edgar wouldn't make it out of the forest alive.

Edgar crawled as fast as he could, his ankle having twisted abnormally around. Through broken sobs and heavy breathing, the more he struggled, the closer the Shape got to him. It raised the knife high into the air, glimmering in the moonlight, and young Edgar saw himself for the last time in the obscured reflection of the blade.

He didn't scream for his mom. He never pleaded

for his life. All ten-year-old Edgar Hugo could manage to push out from deep within his lungs was a loud, panicked, “Ahhhh!”

CHAPTER 1

"Ahhhh, what a bunch of bologna!" Danny Gonz spat at me, one arm slung over his bus seat, his head resting on it.

"Oh yeah, smart guy? It says it right here on the *Wikipedia* page," I shot back and held up my iPhone for Danny to see for himself. "And I know a guy who was at camp at the same time as Edgar Hugo. I'll tell you where he lives and you can ask him yourself!"

The bus was loud, even without all of the kids talking, screaming, and singing throughout. The unpaved road made the ride even more nauseating, especially with the smell of exhaust that constantly hovered above me in the back of the bus.

I scrolled through the *Wikipedia* page on the "Legend of Edgar Hugo," a "See also" from the "Camp Dream Haven" page. This was the last place I wanted to be: crammed into the back of a smelly bus with a bunch of kids I never wanted to hang out with in the first place. I would have rather been at home, kicking it with my squad of real friends playing football. Real football, none of that lame "touch" crap. I wondered for a second if my buddy Tommy Donkers finally figured out the password around the parental control on the Internet. *Now, there's a way to blow through your summer as a fourteen-year-old*, I thought. This should have been the summer where I became a man.

"Okay, TJ. If a kid was murdered by some thing back in ancient times, don't you think there'd be more news stories, or like a statue or something, making it a real thing?" Danny asked. "And why, after all of this time, would Camp Dream Haven *just* be opening back up to the public, hmm? Did they catch the killer? Is he now the new lunch lady?"

Everyone in the back of the bus let out a wild laugh.

"No, I heard that position was given to your mom," I quickly snapped back. "She has to wear a hairnet on her face, though. We can't have beard hairs showing up in our chili." This made Danny sink a little lower in his seat and his smile slowly melted into a grimace.

"Yeah, well everyone knows you're full of it, TJ," Ashley Branca said from a few seats up. "You lie about everything."

"No, I don't . . . " I answered back.

"Oh yeah?" Danny sat back up. "What about the time you told everyone you accidentally got into Kanye West's Uber cab, and he flew you to Paris on his private jet where he was performing a sold-out show, hmm?"

"I had pictures, but my phone was stolen and nothing was backed up on my cloud . . . "

"Or the time you said that you and your dad climbed to the top of Mount Everest with only a backpack and two lines of rope?"

"I seriously couldn't feel my feet for over a week. Do you guys know how cold it gets up there?"

"Or how about when you said that your great-grandpa was some Indian chief who survived a forest fire by just laying in the middle of it all?"

"Wait, now that actually happened . . . "

"It's called an escape fire," a small voice said from a few seats up.

The back of the bus went silent. "What the hell was that?" Danny asked, confused, looking around.

"I personally don't think it's possible, but many Native American cultures believe that becoming one with the elements is a way of avoiding the danger of them all. If you respect it, it respects you."

Everyone in the back few rows looked toward the front of the bus to see who was talking. I felt a sense of relief that the attention was now off of me. A grin grew across my face.

"And how do you know that?" I asked, curious.

A small, timid face revealed itself from behind the bus seat, with her long brown hair framing her big, inquisitive eyes.

"I just read about it right here in my book," she said, holding up the cover for *North American Indian Survival Skills*, her thumb in place to bookmark her spot.

I got up from my seat and made my way up to the girl with the book in hand. "And what are you reading about now?" I asked, figuring out where this was going.

The girl looked up at me warily, but flipped the book open to her current spot anyway. "I'm reading about these rock formations that Native Americans used as a way of communicating in the forest. They would stack up rocks in different ways to tell others where they were, or make landmarks to help guide their people around."

"Why didn't they just leave Post-its on trees like normal people?" Danny asked from his seat.

"Because, dummy, they communicated with the earth around them. These are called cairns. It was like Snapchat back in the day. Native Americans would put them up as a message to their squad letting them know where they were. And they'd go away once the wind blew them over," I answered, while I reached down and grabbed the book. "Do you mind?"

"Well, actually I wasn't really done . . . " The girl said while losing the book.

I thumbed through it without listening to her, walking back to my seat. "Hmm, very interesting," I said sarcastically.

"Was it written by your great-grandpa, TJ?" Danny prodded.

I ignored him. "Reading nature's signs, meat preserving, stealth. This is all crap I had to learn long ago when I had to hang with my Mom's dad every summer as a kid. He is one of the last members of the Chochokpi tribe." I flicked through the pages like it was a flipbook. "This is easy stuff. Why are you reading about this now?" I interrogated the girl. "There's no way you're ever going to use this junk, especially at a daycare like Dream Haven." I looked up from the book and examined her for a few beats. "What's your name? You definitely don't go to school with us."

She took a second to answer. "My name is Madeline. And I don't go to school with you. I was given the opportunity to come to this camp from a counselor I work with."

"You work with a camp counselor?" I asked.

"No . . . " Madeline said reluctantly, "a physical therapy counselor. She's one of the most wonderful people I know. She helps me . . . "

"What type of issues we talking here? Two left feet? A tail we aren't seeing?" I said, then looked back down at Madeline's book.

"You wouldn't understand," Madeline whispered. "Can I have my book back please? It's from the library and I don't really want anything to happen to . . . "

"Mmm," I responded, half-listening to her, while I flipped through the thick textbook. "I'm TJ," I offered while throwing a thumb over my shoulder with my face still in the book. "And this here is Danny Gonz, resident screwball of camp."

Danny gave back a half-hearted salute from his seat and I continued looking at the book. "Do you really think you're going to be building shelters this summer? Or fishing with just the threads of your sweater and a button?" I said and closed up the book. "What makes you think you'll ever need to worry about anything other than wearing enough sunblock and not getting sick from the bug juice at this stupid place?"

Madeline looked down at the filthy bus floor, struggling to make eye contact with anyone around her. She finally let out, "I—I just want to be prepared. If anything happens, I want to know how to handle it. By myself."

The hum and rattle the bus made as it hit every bump and divot on the dusty road rocked the passengers back and forth before it pulled onto the pavement.

"But you're reading . . . during summer," Danny

butted in. "You're basically putting yourself through summer school."

"I . . . " Madeline uttered, "I just like to read."

The entire back of the bus stared at Madeline. Some with their mouths wide open in shock, others grinning slightly at what looked like their new summer prey. Then the laughter started.

"Oh my god. You are so. *Lame.*" Danny said between chuckles.

I finished my laughing fit and placed Madeline's book on top of my lap. "Well, I promise you one thing, Maddy. The only thing you're going to have to survive this summer is boredom. And I'll help you out with the first step."

I opened my window a crack with my thumbs. Then I picked up the book and slipped it out of the window, like it was a twenty-four-hour return slot at the library.

"There, see? Don't you feel better?" I said with a smile. But Maddy's face didn't look mad or angry. She just looked like she lost what was to be her only friend of the summer. "Ahh, what are ya so worried about? Late fees? If there is no book, there are no late fees!"

Danny Gonz did the math in his head. "I don't think that's how it works, dude . . . "

The bus came to a stop as it pulled into a small gas station. The rumble of the engine died and the driver stood up. He pushed out his barely covered belly and stretched out his back. He looked back at the kids, who had stopped talking to hear his address. He wiped the sweat off of his forehead and removed his dirty trucker cap.

"You can get out and stretch your legs, use the bathroom, whatever," he grunted out. "But this bus leaves in ten minutes with or without you back in those seats." He pointed out to three rough-looking men leaning up against the gas station. One spat a black-looking tar out into an empty coffee-grounds tin below him. "I'm sure those fellas can offer a summer just as fun as Camp Dream Haven can. Your choice."

All of the kids filed out of the bus and squinted into the bright afternoon sun. I gave myself a big stretch with both hands locked behind my lower back. I surveyed the area and saw nothing but trees, the paved road, and the gas station.

I saw Maddy break away from the group, doing the best she could at keeping her sadness to herself. I felt bad for what I did, sure. But someone had to be the target that summer. There were no two ways about it, and unfortunately, she was the one who was unwittingly offered up as sacrifice.

But why couldn't I stop looking at her? She was studying a tattered piece of paper stapled a dozen times to a light post. It looked like a wanted sign, beaten up and faded from the weather. It was a picture of a girl, pretty and blond. Smiling, unaware at the moment the photo was snapped that one day she would end up missing. The flyer read: "Missing Person: Amanda Sheridan. DOB: 3/12/1998. Missing since: 6/11/16." *Almost exactly a year ago from today*, I thought to myself.

I broke my gaze from Maddy and found the three men leaning up against the wall were staring at me with blank, vacant looks. I approached them, getting used to walking again.

"Excuse me, gents. I don't suppose you'd be local to this neck of the woods now, would ya?" I asked.

One of the rugged men spat into the tin at my feet. "Reckon you can s'pose that."

I stared at the tin as black tar was oozing down the side. I looked back up at the trio. "Wonderful. I'll be staying around here for a while and I was wondering if you could give me the inside scoop on what's poppin' around here. Any arcades, go-kart tracks? Malls would do, I suppose."

Black Tar spat again, then looked me up and down. "You stayin' at Dream Haven there, then?"

"Why, yes we are!" I replied with a smile. "As you can imagine, being stuck in one place for the summer will get pretty boring after, I don't know, one or two hours. So I'd like to be able to shake it up a bit."

The three looked at each other, speaking sentences

with only their eyes. Black Tar stepped forward. “They opened that camp back up for some reason, but they have no idea what that is inviting, junior.”

I put my hands up, “I mean, we’re just a few kids. It’s not like we’re going to burn the place down.”

“It’s the land—it’s evil. There’s reason why its doors have been hitched closed for so long.” Black Tar got closer to my face. I could smell motor oil and cough drops on his breath. “You do yourself a favor. Stay there together in packs. Don’t you ever split up, now.” He then looked dead into my eyes. “And if there is anything you do not do, it’s going out into them woods.”

My heart beat a tad faster at this advice and the seriousness he said it with. The engine of the bus roared to a start and the horn blared loud into the lot, bringing me back to reality. The bus driver leaned out of the driver-side window.

“Bus is movin’. Let’s go!”

CHAPTER 2

I GOT UP, MINUS THE BOOK I STARTED THE TRIP with, and made my way to the back exit of the bus. The bus had just pulled under a big wooden sign that read, WELCOME TO CAMP DREAM HAVEN! The wood was new and the paint was fresh, like it was still drying. From inside the bus, I saw new and kind faces, some scurrying around, making sure everything was just right—others were already lined up in a row near where the bus pulled to a stop. Everyone was wearing the same powder-blue T-shirt with a big Camp Dream Haven logo on the front.

The bus came to a complete stop and everyone got

up at the same time. Some went directly to the front while others went out the back emergency door that was opened by one of the blue T-shirts. I stayed put in my seat waiting for that group of jerks who hassled me earlier to be as far away from the bus as possible.

"Hey there! We're so glad you're here!" said the blue T-shirt who couldn't have been older than seventeen years old. "My name is Andrew. But you can call me Cahak. I'm in charge of music programming."

"Saw-hawk? Is that Native American?" I asked, looking down at him from the exit door.

"Sounds like it, doesn't it?" he said and reached up for my hand. I only stared at it for a few seconds.

"It's okay, I can get down myself," I said slowly, lowering myself off of the back of the bus.

"Suit yourself. As for my name, it's from the Czech Republic, I think. That's just the way the name is pronounced: Saw-hawk," he said as he gave me room to get down. "As you'll notice around here this summer, not everything is as it seems."

I stared at TJ from across the big grassy opening as

he yukked it up and punched one of the other boys in the shoulder. He wasn't the tallest of the boys at camp, but he stood confidently. Without breaking my gaze, I responded, "Yeah, I'm starting to get that impression."

Cahak looked down at me and saw that I was lost in thought. "Hey, I know these things are kind of scary at first. I was terrified the first summer I went to camp, too."

I looked up at him. "Really?"

"Oh yeah, sure! You're in a different place. You probably don't know many people. You feel like maybe you're lost in a big forest and can't find your way out, right?"

I observed the freshly cut grass below my shoes. "You can say that again."

"Well, I'll give you some advice a counselor gave to me the first night I spent at camp. If something scares you, it means it's probably worth it." He held out my duffel bag to take, but I just looked at it.

"Uh, you can just leave it on the ground for now. I'll pick it up in a second."

Cahak noticed me slowly covering my hands with my faded pink and gray hoodie sleeves. "Yeah, sure. No problem." He carefully placed my duffel bag on the ground and closed up the trailer hitched to the bus. "Say, go around the bus to where those people are standing." At his insistence, I peeked my head around the bus to see three people, one adult and two teenagers, standing together. "The guy wearing the safari hat and white gunk on his nose is the camp director, Mr. Venkman. I'm sure he'd like to meet you."

I turned back to Cahak. "Okay. Thanks for the help."

Cahak smiled. "Any time. Just call out for Saw-hawk and I'll be there."

I turned around and marched towards Mr. Venkman, who was in the middle of a conversation with the two teen counselors.

"I know that, but we aren't canceling the rafting

trip. Not now. They just got here for Pete's sake, and we're going to start the summer by disappointing the kids? Not on my watch."

"But Mr. Venkman, there's too much at risk here. Some of the counselors aren't that familiar with the river, or comfortable for that matter . . . " said the female counselor.

"This is the first day, and we're already disagreeing? It has taken thirty years to get this place up and going again after several dozen road bumps that have kept it from opening. One mistake and it's going to look like we were not ready, or we aren't competent enough to run this place." Venkman breathed in. "The quarry is not scheduled to do the expansion for another week. Just stick to the maps you were given and . . . " Venkman noticed me walking up to them. "We'll finish discussing this later."

"Hi, Mr. Venkman? My name is Madeline. Madeline Olstad. I was actually sent up here by . . . "

"Ah, yes! Madeline Olstad. It was suggested by your therapist, Ms. Newman, to come join us for the summer. And might I be the first to say, we are so glad you're here!"

"Well, Cahak actually was the first to say that to me," I answered bashfully.

"Great! We're paying him for *something* then. Let me introduce you to our two program directors here at Camp Dream Haven." Mr. Venkman pointed to the two teens next to him. "Here we have Jack Kooy, he programs the arts and crafts you'll be doing each day."

Jack had narrow, bright blue eyes and short, messed-up blond hair to go with them. A puka shell necklace snugly hugged his neck. "Hey there! Madeline, right?"

"Yep, Madeline. But you can call me Maddy."

"It's nice to meet you, Maddy! Do you like making art at all?"

"Oh, yes very much. I have a sketchbook that I keep with me at all times. I really like to watercolor," I responded.

"That's awesome! Wait until you see the sunset up

here. The mix of soft pink and purple across the sky will give you a great picture to add to your book."

A woman in her mid-seventies walked up to us from out of nowhere. Her curled white hair and the spectacles that dangled in front of her canary-yellow polo did not match the tattoo sleeves she had on each arm. "We're out of aloe vera and we don't have enough cortizone to last us the summer," she grunted at Venkman, unaware, or frankly uninterested, about interrupting the conversation.

"The budget is in place for a reason," Venkman replied sternly. "Madeline, this is Ms. Patrick. She is the resident nurse here at Camp Dream Haven."

I smiled, "Hi, Ms. Patrick."

Ms. Patrick observed me for a moment. "You don't have to worry about that Ms. Patrick stuff. You can call me what everyone else calls me: Buzz."

"They call you Buzz?" I asked.

Unless I imagined it, Buzz grew half an inch of a smile out of the side of her mouth. "They call me Buzz because my office is the only place on the grounds where you'll find a phone. Even if you were allowed cell phones up here, you wouldn't get a lick of service this deep in the woods."

"Right," Venkman interjected. "Madeline is here on suggestion from her therapist. She should be on the list for daily medication."

Buzz looked at the crumpled, stapled stack of paper in her hands. "Madeline June Olstad. Age fourteen. I have you down daily for nonsteroidal anti-inflammatories, Trexall and Rituxan. Is that right?"

"That'll do it," I answered.

"Well come see me after you're done here. We'll get you set up for the rest of the day," said Buzz, who did an about-face and walked away.

"Bye, Buzz," Jack called out.

"Nice to meet you, Buzz," I followed.

Buzz gave a wave over her shoulder. Another camper passed her by saying, "Hi, Buzz."

Venkman hopped back in and pointed to the female counselor, "Right, well then. This here is

Telly Bernel. She runs the sports and activities side of camp."

Telly warmly waved, "Hi there." She was tall, olive-skinned, and athletic. It was like she came right out of one of my books on all-time great Olympic athletes.

Venkman continued, "Both Telly and Jack started out as campers just like you are now. Of course it was at a different camp, but I trusted them enough to help me get Dream Haven up and going again. Maybe one day you'll be a counselor here with them!"

I looked between the counselors and directors, but didn't say anything.

"Is everything okay?" Telly asked.

I took a second and then snapped back into the conversation. "Hmm? Oh, yeah. It was just . . . " I watched as TJ pretended to push a girl off of the dock. " . . . It was just a long bus ride is all. I'm kind of tired."

Telly looked over her shoulder at the ruckus by the dock and then back to me. "I think I understand.

Jack, can you grab Madeline's bag and show her to Buzz's office, please?" She looked at the clipboard she was holding. "She's in Hemlock Bunk."

Jack bent down, picked up the duffel, and saluted Telly at the same time. "Aye, aye, Captain!"

Telly walked away toward the dock, leaving me with Jack.

■ ■ ■

I saw my older sister, Telly, marching towards the squad and me on the dock. I'd felt like I'd be able to spend the summer avoiding her. Luck, as it seemed, was not on my side.

Telly approached the dock, crammed with preteen boys, one of which was me, in the middle of the mayhem. The loud screams and laughter turned into hushed whispers.

"Here she comes, TJ."

"Shut up! Shh, I'll tell you later," I murmured to Danny Gonz. "Uh oh, guys. Here come the fun police," I announced, and gave a stiff salute. The squad behind me snickered.

Telly stood tall in front of the pack of animals staring her down. "Daniel, I believe they need you to help back at your bunk. Go up there and give them a hand."

Danny crossed his arms and nodded toward the bunks, "Looks like they're doing fine without me." He slipped me some skin.

Telly broke her stare down with me without moving her head and pointed it at Danny. "Get up there or I'll get Mrs. Gonzales on the phone, and you can talk about it with her on the ride home."

Without a word, Danny was halfway to the bunks within a few quick steps.

Telly looked at the rest of the boys, save for yours truly. "Do you mind? I'd like to talk to my brother for a second." A long silence lapsed. "Alone."

The crowd brushed past her, all whispering and laughing. I watched as my last line of defense left just me and my older sister alone, standing on the dock.

The wind was the only thing between her and me as neither of us said a word.

■ ■ ■

"Hey, hi. Yeah, it's me, Maddy," I spoke into the phone on Buzz's wall.

"Hi, Junebug! How is it? Are you having a blast or what?"

I chuckled softly. "Jeez, Mom, I've only been here for ten minutes. Let me get a feel for the place first before I start writing up my Yelp review."

We both laughed, but I could hear Mom sigh softly on the other side of the phone. I had never been away from her for such a long period of a time. Not after Mom's accident, that is. "Am I missing anything back at home?"

"Dexter tore the trash open all over the kitchen and ate a mountain's worth of raw chicken. And Jacob was suspended from his football game because he mooned Sibley High's head coach on the way to the game." She took a breath. "Teddy, Peter, Neil, and Max are off doing God knows what with God knows who. But those are your brothers for you. Other than that, the ship is in fine shape."

I twirled the phone cord around my index finger, watching my finger go from red to white to purple. Like holding my breath for too long, then releasing it, my finger went back to its normal color. I'd done that ever since I was a little kid. It helped me focus on something else even when I was stressing out. "Have you heard from him at all?"

A silence filled the phone line. "Only through the letters his attorney sends me and the slew of bills coming in the mail. But I want it like that. It's best for you and your brothers that we don't hear from him. It's better this way."

A single tear rolled down my cheek. I let it make it to my chin before wiping it away with my faded gray-and-pink hoodie sleeve. "Yeah, it's better this way."

Mom turned the cheer up in her voice to change

the course of the conversation. "So, what's on the agenda for today?"

I sniffled once and wiped another tear away, not doing so hot on turning the cheer up on my end. "Um, I have to unpack and meet my cabin mates. Then we have some swimming test to see if we're strong enough swimmers for the summer."

"I remember reading about that. Swimming is good! You can do that no sweat, right?"

"Yeah, it doesn't bother me. Ms. Newman said it won't affect my joints and it's good exercise." I twisted the cord around my wrist this time. "Mom?"

"Yeah, my Junebug?"

I wanted to simply say "I love you." I wanted to tell my mom that I was scared. Petrified, actually. I wanted to come home and be there to help with our big dummy of a dog, Dexter. I wanted to be there at night when mom usually began to cry. I wanted to be strong for mom and for myself—but right then I knew that I couldn't. I couldn't even say "I love you."

All I could muster was, “I have to go, I’ll try to call you later in the week.”

“Okay, Junebug. Be sure to check your mailbox whenever you can. I’ll be sending letters. And I’ll see what I can do about putting money into your canteen fund. I’m sorry I couldn’t do that before you left.”

“Don’t apologize. I don’t need anything from there.”

“Well, I want you to have the best summer you can. So don’t forget to take your medicine, or you won’t have a very good time at all.”

“I won’t,” I said. “Bye, Mom.”

■ ■ ■

Telly broke the silence first. “How was the bus ride?”

I didn’t say anything. I just continued to stare past her.

“Make any new friends?”

I finally looked at her. “It was a freaking bus ride. What do you want me to say?” I looked down at the

Astroturf-covered dock. "At least you got to drive up here on your own. You didn't have to sit on a crummy bus full of mouth breathers drooling all over you for five hours."

"You wouldn't have even *been* on that bus or up here at all if you'd just acted like a normal human being for once in your life." She said this without breaking her laser focus on me. "What, do you think this is some sort of punishment or something?"

I spat off of the dock and watched the loogie island float in the lake for a few seconds before I came up with my response. "Getting forced onto a bus and being dumped off in the middle of Hicksville for the summer? Yeah, I'd say this is a punishment."

Telly let out a little frustrated laugh. "Oh, so washing the church windows with Pepsi wasn't your fault?"

I smirked at that memory. The syrup in the pop stained the glass a caramel brown throughout the church. The custodian had to stay back three extra hours to clean it up. That was a good one.

Anger crept into Telly's voice. "And I suppose the Porta-Potty in the park burned itself down, right?"

That actually wasn't my idea at all. Joe Mulvehill, the class prankster, came up with that jewel of a plan. He had mentioned during Social Studies that a great gag to pull on people is to light something on fire and toss it into an empty Porta-Potty. That way, when the next person to use the can opened the door, they would get a face full of smoke. No harm, no foul.

Once my mom was finally out of the house one sunny afternoon, Tom Donkers and I collected all of the dryer lint we could find and put it in a Ziploc bag. We brought the bag to Erlandson Park, the only place we knew where a Porta-Potty existed. Tom flicked his lighter a few times before the flame came out to where I held the lint. Before we knew it, it was on fire and inside of the smelly plastic toilet. With the door shut, we jogged away in a fury of laughter, imagining the poor sap who would be the one to open that door.

Fifteen minutes later, unable to control the urge to check on our handiwork, Tom and I moseyed back to the scene of the crime—a classic, rookie arsonist mistake—to see the big, green tower completely engulfed in flames. In a panic, I tried to scoop water out of a nearby puddle to subdue the fire while Tom filmed it for Snapchat.

"World Star!" Tom sang loudly with one hand holding the phone while the other made a sideways peace sign in the air.

I stared into the phone hysterically while limply tossing half a handful of water onto the flames. "Will you put that down and help me, you big ape?!"

Unfortunately, that was when the police showed up.

"That was supposed to be a controlled burn. It just got . . . out of control. That's all," I quipped sarcastically.

The patience in Telly had run dry. "Okay. But what about what happened with dad, huh?" This dug deep into me. I didn't say a word, only looking directly into Telly's eyes while mine filled up with tears. "Are you just going to call that a freak accident?"

I said all I needed to say without having to utter a single word.

Telly saw this. She scoffed, looked away for a second, then brought it back to me. "Don't you get it, you stupid little jerk? This isn't a punishment. None of us are punishing you. It's only you punishing yourself. We had to get you away—we had to save you from you."

The wind in the air and the birds in the trees were the only ones doing the talking, as I had nothing to say.

Telly turned away and started walking towards the bunks. She stopped after a few steps and turned back around one last time. "You lit this fuse, TJ." I finally looked up at her. "Now deal with the explosion."

CHAPTER 3

I MADE MY WAY TO THE HEMLOCK BUNK FROM Buzz's office, where I had taken my medicine and called Mom. The screen door made a strained creaking sound as I pulled it open with a closed fist. The bunk was empty, as everyone had already left without me for the swimming test.

Jack had delivered my bag as promised, and it was sitting on the only unmade bed in the room. I pushed the duffel off of the mattress with my shoulder and watched as it fell to the ground. I picked up my military-green sleeping bag and rolled it out perfectly over the stained, thin mattress. Jacob, my second to oldest brother, had always had a thing for the army—he was going to kill me when he realized that I'd taken the sleeping bag without telling him.

Bending down, I unzipped my duffel and started sifting through the clothes that were once folded nicely by mom and were now a sea of wrinkles and chaos contained within the bag. The screen door slamming shut behind me broke my concentration.

"Oh, I didn't think anyone was in here," said a girl I recognized from the bus. She looked me over. "You're the book girl from the bus. Madeline, right?"

"Yeah, but you can call me Maddy."

"Nice to meet you! I'm Ashley," she said, not moving from the door. "Are you going to come swim with us?"

I looked down at the bathing suit I was holding in my hand then back up to Ashley, who was already wearing hers. "Yeah, I just wanted to get myself organized before I headed down there." I slowly pulled the sleeve of my faded gray and pink hoodie over my other hand.

Ashley noticed me doing that immediately. "What's wrong with your hands?"

This caught me off-guard, as I'd never had anyone straight up ask me about my issue before this. Usually people made me feel more like a freak by addressing the problem in awkward ways, like pretending it's not even there.

"I'm sorry. I shouldn't have . . . " Ashley recognized. "I have this issue where I have to say everything I think of. My dad says I have 'train brain.' Like nothing will stop it."

We both laughed. I decided to drop my swimsuit onto the military-green sleeping bag, and stretched out my arms so my hands were free from the faded sleeves.

"It's okay," I said, holding my hands up to Ashley. As long as I can remember, my knuckles have been beet-red, swollen, and puffy. Both of my pinkies have always pointed inwards toward the rest of my fingers. And the ring finger on my left hand is shorter than the rest of them in line. "I have juvenile arthritis."

"Whoa, have your hands always been like that?" Ashley asked as she examined my hands up close without touching them.

"Kind of. It started off like nothing, then as the years went on it got worse. It's just something I have to deal with every day. I'm here because my therapist said being here with kids not like me will help. I think my therapist wants me to feel 'normal' or something . . . whatever that is."

Ashley looked up from my hands to me. "I don't think we're very different." I smiled at this. "Come on, suit up. We have to do this swimming thing. You can swim, right?"

I dropped my hands and picked the bathing suit back up. "Yep, I love swimming."

"Well, what are you waiting for? We gotta see if you are brave enough to swim in the deep end, or if you're a baby and need to stay on shore with your floaties."

"Okay, okay!" I said through a smothered giggle. "I'll be down in a minute."

Ashley turned around and cracked the screen door open to leave.

"Hey, Ashley . . . " I called out.

"Yeah?" Ashley said, turning around.

"That kid—TJ. What's his problem?"

"Oh, we all have problems."

"Yeah, I know. But am I going to have to deal with him all summer? Like, have to put up with his crap?"

Ashley gave me a warm smile. "Don't worry about him. That kid is so full of hot air he could be a whoopee cushion. He spins big talk to impress his 'squad' or whatever and tries to look tough. But if you keep your distance and let him find another target, you should be fine."

I took in the advice.

"You're going to hear a lot of stories about him. Most are pure crap. You can never tell with someone like him."

"What kind of stories?" I asked.

"Mostly stuff he likes to make up to seem cool.

Others that he doesn't want to talk about, but people know anyways."

This piqued my curiosity. "Like what?"

Ashley pushed the screen door open wider, letting the sun drape the wooden floors of the cabin, leaving her in a dark silhouette. "Like the fact that he killed his dad."

■ ■ ■

I craned my head to look around the Hemlock cabin. *Finally*, I thought to myself as I watched Maddy exit down the steps toward the docks in her swimsuit. It was now or never.

"So, tell me what we're doing again, TJ?" Danny asked over my shoulder.

I gave an annoyed half-turn to face Danny. "Just keep your yap shut and follow my lead. The *plan* is to make this summer as fun as possible—even if we have to burn this dump to the ground."

"I still don't understand what is going on right

now," Jimmy Kreager piped up from behind Danny. Jimmy was a junior counselor. He was tall, skinny, impossibly pale, and always wearing skinny jeans with a black hooded zip-up. He was a year older than me and Danny, but he'd always thought of us as the cool kids. This could be his only chance to break in with our crowd. And I knew it, obviously going to take advantage of having a man on "the inside" if we needed it.

I looked around the corner again. "Of course you don't, Jimmy. You think you're a freaking vampire." The coast was finally clear. "All right, let's go."

The screen door creaked then held silent as our three bodies piled awkwardly into the cabin. An odd feeling came across me, like I was in an environment that I had no business being in. Like a haunted insane asylum or rooting around in my uncle's office desk. The atmosphere just felt different—like the smells were sweeter and the light was brighter. It made me physically uncomfortable.

All three of us looked around the cabin and tried

to find something. Anything. What it was, I hadn't figured out. That was until a bright glimmer came across my eyes. "Bingo."

■ ■ ■

There was a big splash with a moment of screams and cheers, then silence. Screams, cheers, then silence. Screams, cheers, silence.

I made it back to the dock and was helped out of the water by Cahak. Everyone around me applauded as I draped a towel over my shoulders. The wind was heavy, carrying leaves and making the tree branches sway above us.

The swift change from the cold of the lake to the warmth of the sun had caused goose bumps to form all over my body. If the feeling of immense happiness at that moment didn't mean that I was truly alive, then I couldn't really explain the stupid grin that was plastered wide across my face.

"You are a really strong swimmer!" Cahak said, scribbling onto his clipboard.

I wiped a little bit of snot from my nose with my towel-wrapped fist. "Thanks! I've been swimming ever since I was three." I quaked a little from the chill of the breeze. "It's practically the only thing I can do physically."

"Well, we'll see about that," Cahak said, finishing up his notes then looking back up at me. "There's plenty more to explore this summer. Excellent job!"

Ashley gave me a huge thumbs-up, and I threw back a towel-covered thumb at her—until something floating in the water caught my attention. What was it? A pink fish? That couldn't have been . . . it looked far too familiar.

The rest of the kids on the dock stepped closer to the edge to inspect what was floating up and down within the lake as well. I got down on my knees, trying to see if it was truly what I had thought it was. *No—no, it can't possibly be . . .*

"That's my underwear!" I shrieked while fishing it

out of the water. "How, but . . . why?" I stood up and hid my underwear under the towel I had dropped.

The kids, who a moment ago were cheering me on, were slowly beginning to snicker.

"Okay, everyone relax. This is just an accident," Cahak said, trying to bring order back to the dock. "It must have been mistakenly brought down here with the towel or something. Nothing to laugh at."

The second Cahak put a period to that sentence, he was smacked in the face with what looked like a training bra. Surely that could have been a mere coincidence. That could have been a camp-wide epidemic, where random laundry had been picked up in a freak storm and tossed around for all to see. Surely I wasn't the only victim of that flood of embarrassment.

That was until Cahak peeled the cotton and Lycra off of his face, revealing the bold "Olstad" embroidered on the strap. I had always loved that mom did that for me. Having not much to call my own, it made it feel like the piece of clothing was mine and only mine. That day, however, may have taken the polish off of that idea all together.

"I, uh—" Cahak sheepishly said as he handed it to me. With my face the shade of Santa Claus's jacket, I reached out and took it from him. "Did you leave the cabin door open or something?"

Everyone on the dock save for Cahak and me were now laughing in hysterics.

"I have no idea what is going on here . . . " I said while noticing a T-shirt, pair of shorts, and blouse that were at one point in my duffel bag tumble down the hill toward the dock with the wind. "That's more of my stuff!"

I left the dock while everyone followed behind as I gathered the breadcrumbs of my clothes. A sock, another pair of underwear, and scrunchies were what I gathered from the grass until I finally looked up and saw it.

"Ahh—son of a . . . " I whispered under my breath.

The flagpole. The forty-five-foot-tall pillar directly

in the middle of the camp. The pole that at one point had the American flag gallantly streaming, which was now replaced with all of my clothes. What seemed like half of the camp was out there staring, shielding their eyes from the sun as if they were saluting the vertical clothesline flapping in the wind. One could swear they heard a bald eagle fly by at the exact moment my PJ bottoms broke free of the rope and fluttered towards the woods.

More people started piling out of their cabins, with campers already laughing and counselors rushing to the flagpole. I watched in utter horror while they brought my whole summer wardrobe down to half-mast, then completely to the ground. Through all of the embarrassment, my attention was brought to the Mess Hall, the building where they serve the meals, and saw TJ with his band of flunkies saunter out wearing bright smiles . . . smiles of the pride they felt about their latest work of art.

Our stares met for a brief moment. *I know it was you*, I said through my squinted eyes, while TJ's stare simply stated *innocent until proven guilty*. That tore it. And so I rushed toward the Mess Hall.

"What in the hell is your problem?!" I screamed to TJ. "What did I do? What is it that you can't stand about me?"

TJ looked around in a faux state of confusion. "Lady, I have no idea what you're going on about."

"Yes you do—you did this! I know you did!"

Telly and Jack walked up to the Mess Hall patio where the yelling was happening.

"What is going on here?" Telly pointedly interrogated TJ. He just shrugged and threw his arms in the air.

"I was having fun. I was beginning to make friends. I finally had a chance to feel good about myself, and so you wanted to make sure that didn't happen, right? It bothers you to see other people happy, doesn't it?"

Telly pulled me back because there was enough heat generating off of me to power a steamboat.

"Just tell me it bothers you, you jerk!"

"Okay, okay. Let's calm down a second," Telly said calmly trying to diffuse the situation. "TJ, how did those clothes get up there?"

TJ had stepped forward. "Couldn't tell ya," he said while he pointed to his friends. "We were in the Mess Hall, getting it ready for tonight. You know, for dinner and the counselor skits? Our supervisor, James Kreager here, can place us there during the raising of our camp's new flag."

Telly looked at the teenage vampire. "Jim, is this true?"

Jim didn't say anything. He just looked from face to face and then nodded under his hood.

I struggled out of Telly's hands and stormed off, collecting the rest of my clothes as I stomped back towards Hemlock Bunk.

■ ■ ■

"If I find out you had *anything* to do with this . . . " Telly said, going nose-to-nose with me.

"You'll do what? Send me home?" I piped up hopefully.

Telly snorted. "Fat chance. That's exactly what you're trying to do. I can see through you like cellophane." She got closer, nearly pushing my nose sideways with hers. "If I find out you had anything to do with this, I'll make sure you spend every summer here until the day you die." She jabbed her long, bony index finger into my chest. "You'll be the freaking camp director of this place by the time I'm through with you."

I became overly confused as to whether that was a threat or not. "You got it, sis." I turned back to the boys. "Let's blow." We all turned around in unison and walked back into the Mess Hall, letting the screen door slam shut behind us.

■ ■ ■

Night fell, and everyone was in the Mess Hall,

laughing, eating, and playing with their food. Well, everyone but me.

"You liking the food at least, Maddy?" Cahak asked while walking past the table, his hands full with his own tray. I looked up and plastered a semi-smile on my face, followed by a nod.

The counselors and junior counselors all did a few different skits earlier in the evening, like what you should and shouldn't do while at Dream Haven—Bug spray, yes. Bug spray near the campfire, no. They also ran through a couple of songs that the campers would be singing throughout the summer—one about doing something called the "Popsicle," another about a slippery fish.

And at the end, all of the counselors got on stage and performed a skit about the history of Camp Dream Haven. Founded in 1912 by Juliette Gordon Ward, it originally started off as a Girl Scout camp, where girls would learn about their strengths, passions, and talents. Ms. Ward felt strongly that the girls of the future generations were the ones who would indeed grow up and change the world for the better. Unfortunately, in 1951, boys knocked on the camp door and ruined the party.

But for thirty long years, the camp made many summers special for thousands of children. Dream Haven isn't a place just to have fun, excitement, and adventure—but a place to truly figure out who you are, inside and out. Or so they said.

I sat quietly at the end of my table and occasionally looked up to find people from across the room still pointing and whispering. They had already got a good look at my literal dirty laundry, so what else could they possibly be talking about? I looked down and tuned back into my fish sticks.

"TJ is so thirsty," Ashley said, nudging me with her elbow. "He's just like this at school. He finds someone weak . . . " I looked up at Ashley, who tried to slow her train brain down. "That's not what I meant. He just always has to go out of his way to make someone feel bad about themselves. It's like his style, if there was such a thing," she said, thinking about it. "Thirstcore is what it'd be called."

I broke a small smile out of the side of my mouth, trying my best to keep my frown intact.

"Listen, this is only the first day. We have the rest of the summer to have a blast."

I dropped my soggy fish stick down onto my plate. "And how in the hell are we supposed to do that if I'm gonna be in the crosshairs of some lunatic all summer?"

Ashley got closer to my ear and lowered her voice. "About that . . . I think I have an idea."

CHAPTER 4

THE BONFIRES WERE ROARING OUTSIDE, WITH sparks flying into the sky, getting lost in the sea of stars. There were rows of fire pits, each one surrounded by a dozen campers and one or two counselors. The smell of bug spray and bonfire smoke combined into a scent one can only describe as a "true summer night."

I was sitting by Ashley, my only friend at the moment, while we watched that Danny Gonz kid tell a "ghost story."

"He crawled as fast as he could. But his ankle, you know, it was twisted, right?" Danny said, standing before the great, blazing fire. He used his hands for extra theatrical effect. "But this thing, whatever it was, kept coming at him. Like, super savage. But no matter what, Edgar Hugo couldn't get his frail body up and moving again."

Everyone around the campfire hung onto every word, some not blinking for whole minutes at a time.

"The thing got closer, and before Edgar knew it, the thing that was hunting him was hovering over him. The thing that was like, about to kill him . . . broke out into this *fire* freestyle rap. Like, they needed to call the fire department, he was spitting so much heat."

The audience relaxed and began to laugh at this idiot's tale that had gone off of the rails.

"And if you listen hard enough, some say you can still hear that dude's insane freestyle echo in the woods."

Everyone began to applaud Danny as he took his bows and sat back down by TJ.

"Very nice . . . story there, Daniel," Telly said, still seated.

One of the other girls from the Hemlock Bunk, Emily Poindexter, raised her hand slightly. "That story, the real one. About that kid—Edgar Hugo. Is it true? Is that why this place closed down so long ago?"

Telly smiled. "Of course not. The 'legend' of Edgar Hugo is about as real as my brother TJ beating Jordan Spieth in nine holes of golf."

"I did get him on the 'closest to the pin' contest, though," TJ responded without cracking a smile.

Telly rolled her eyes and continued. "Every camp has a story like Edgar Hugo's. People like to come up with things like that because they want to scare kids like you. It isn't enough that a summer can actually be fun without worrying for your life. You add an element of danger to the story, and you make it much more exciting."

"What about the case of Amanda Sheridan?" said Jack, who walked up to the fire and dropped an armload of wood to the ground.

"Who is Amanda Sheridan?" I asked.

"Well, Maddy, she was in the news a while back, before they even considered opening this place back up. She went kayaking down the Packer River one summer day—and was never to be heard of again," Jack said through a sick smile accentuated by the firelight. "It was like she vanished into thin air."

"Was it the same monster that got Edgar Hugo?" Danny asked from behind his hooded sweatshirt that was covering his mouth.

"No," Telly insisted while throwing a marshmallow at Jack. "Whatever happened to her had absolutely nothing to do with monsters or the camp closing."

"So . . . why was the camp closed, then?" Emily asked.

"Honestly, the story is boring. It has to do with businessmen, land deals, and a rock quarry that no one wanted to expand," Telly quickly explained. "But everything worked out. The businessmen are allowed to do what they want with the quarry, even if it will make the air a lot more polluted, and this land is now back open."

"So the real story is a lot scarier than the tale of Edgar Hugo," TJ chimed back in.

"We don't have to worry about the pollution that comes with the expansion. The quarry is at least fifteen miles from Camp Dream Haven," Telly continued. "This expanse of land was just a part of a tug-of-war for money that happened for a long, long time. Once they got it, we got to have our summers back."

Everyone around the fire became quiet, not quite knowing how to feel about the true history of the place. We all let the crackle and dance of the fire have the stage for a brief moment.

"Okay, well let's hear some *real* stories now," Telly said and clapped her hands together. "Who has one that they want to share? Like something to do with being brave or surviving in the woods."

"What about the one TJ always tells," Danny suggested from his chair. "About your great-great-grandpa surviving being burned alive in a forest fire."

"He didn't burn alive, dumb dumb, he survived the forest fire by being smart," TJ spat back.

Telly laughed. "Shocking as it is, this story is a true one my grandpa heard from his father, who heard it from his father before him."

This grabbed the attention of the circle. Telly moved closer to the fire, close enough that you could see the reflection of the flames in her eyes. "Our great-great-grandfather was the last remaining member of the Chochokpi Indian tribe. He took incredible pride in his heritage, passing the culture down to our great-grandfather, who passed it down to our grandfather, and so on. One evening, he was coming home from a vision quest, which he did often. It was essentially spending a long time alone with no distractions to help you find yourself."

"You can do it now-a-days in your room playing *Call of Duty*," TJ interrupted, gaining a weak chuckle.

You could tell from the look on his face that the response was less than what he was hoping for.

Telly just ignored him. "He was walking back to his village on a very dry night by himself. A lightning storm had moved in on the territory and eventually a bolt hit a particularly dried-out mess of woods, lighting them up like a Christmas tree."

The fire in front of us acted like a perfect visual aid to her story. "He was surrounded by walls of flames everywhere he turned, without an exit in sight. The only option he really had left was to create an escape fire."

"What's an escape fire?" Emily eagerly asked.

"Well, the Chochokpi believe power lies within the earth itself. So what he did was find a piece of land that was already burnt down. He got down on his knees, surrounded himself in the ash, and laid face-first in the earth."

Telly let that hang in the air for everyone to imagine.

"So . . . what happened?!" Danny demanded to know.

"Well, the fire just passed right over him," Telly replied.

"Just like that?!"

"Just like that."

"Whoa."

"Scientifically, it works because the ashes and earth he surrounded himself with offered nothing for the fire to eat, basically. It was already all chewed up. But what he and his people believed was that he was showing reverence to the earth. He respected her. So she protected him."

The crackle and pop of the fire in front of us continued the story, if only briefly—then TJ made a loud farting noise with his two hands over his mouth. That got the reaction of laughter he wanted from the crowd. A banner ending to his performance for the evening.

■ ■ ■

Through the laughter and flames, I noticed two girls leaving the bonfire under rather suspicious circumstances. Ashley and that Maddy chick. It would have been one thing if they were just going to the bathroom together. Girls do that for some reason; the john must be a scary place to them, I guessed. But, no—they left at an opportune moment, when no one was paying attention to them. Nobody does that unless they have a good reason to. If anyone knew that, it was me. And not knowing what that reason was left me wanting answers.

■ ■ ■

"Okay, so what's this bright idea?" I asked as I followed Ashley into the cabin.

Ashley turned around, a bright smile between two maps she held up with both hands. "I found the original map that the guides are going to use for our rafting trip tomorrow."

"Yeah, so?"

"Yeah, so? Do you see anything different about this one?" Ashley asked, shaking the one map in her left hand.

"Yeah—this one takes a drastically different route than the one on the right." I thought for a few seconds until it finally clicked. "Wait, we're going to send his raft down the wrong path?"

Ashley gave a devious smile and nodded up and down at me.

"Oh, I don't know . . . " I nervously replied. "This could be going too far. What if someone gets hurt or they get lost for good?"

"It's no big deal! I did the math, they'll only get diverted by a few miles. There won't be much more than a few hours of being turned around and possibly a hike back to camp."

I didn't say anything, but wore a worried look on my face. Ashley picked up on this quickly.

"It's only been a day here and he's already put the full-court press on making your life hell, right?"

"Yeah, but—"

"Think about it, if you want the respect of the yard, you need to take down the big dog, right?"

"I don't know about any of that—"

"Think about everyone who he's ever tormented for no reason. Think of everyone that hasn't had the opportunity to stick it to him like we have right here. We could be legends after this."

"Okay, I honestly think—"

"And if he knows what we're capable of—what you're capable of—he won't be so quick to strike back now, will he?"

I looked Ashley deep in the eyes to see if she was being serious. She was. Ashley very much was.

"That does make a lot of sense," I conceded.

"I knew you'd come around!"

"Okay, so what's the plan?"

"Simple. Jack is their bunk guide tomorrow, yeah? We just swap the map out of his pack and replace it with this one. We do it right before we take off in the morning when everyone is distracted. That way, no witnesses, no blame."

"TJ will know it was us," I warned.

"Oh," Ashley proclaimed. "I'm really counting on it."

"Why?" I finally had to ask. "What stakes do you have in this?"

Ashley bit her lip and looked away for a brief second. "I get it."

"Get what?" I questioned, still confused.

Ashley sighed. "Let's just say I was on TJ's list of targets long enough to realize people like him never learn, unless someone truly teaches them a lesson."

Silence filled the space between us until I nodded in agreement. The plan was in place.

We left the cabin, freshly invigorated with the idea that we would finally get ours. With the help of my accomplice, I would finally end my time as low-level outsider-reject the next morning. Things were going to be different. And we were going to make that so.

The morning was bright and hot, without a hint of wind. They had said a thunderstorm was coming, but it wouldn't arrive until hours after our trip. Everyone scurried around to make sure they had everything they needed before embarking on our daylong adventure. Counselors packed up the back of each of the vans that would be taking the campers to the riverbank where we would start our journey.

I stepped out of Buzz's office, holding onto my backpack by one strap. Buzz followed behind.

"Now, remember Maddy, that's a day's worth of your medication in there. You shouldn't have to use it all, so whatever you have left be sure to bring back to me."

I slung my *One-Punch Man* backpack over one shoulder. "I feel fine. I don't think they are letting me do anything crazy physical on this trip. This shouldn't be a problem."

Buzz looked me in the eyes. "You remember the twelve-spoon rule, don't you?"

I rolled my eyes because I had recited it a million times before. "Yes. I start off every day with twelve spoons of energy. Everything I do requires at least one spoon from me."

"And when you're out of those spoons?" Buzz quizzed.

"Then it's time for me to rest up and recharge those spoons." I answered.

"That's right. Remember, a raft is like a ship," Buzz declared. "Everyone ought to be prepared to take the helm."

"It's 'a *community* is like a ship,'" Telly interjected while walking by with her arms full.

Buzz watched as she walked by. "Just be sure to take them at the right time and everything should be smooth sailing."

"I will," I complied, swinging the other strap onto my bare shoulder. From across the lawn, I watched as Ashley slipped the folded white map out of Jack's knapsack that was sitting outside of a van—and replaced it with the map she had tucked in the back of her jean shorts. Once the deed was done, Ashley looked around for any witnesses and then jogged away to help someone lift a cooler into the back of another van. "Thanks, Buzz."

I walked up to one of the vans and threw my backpack into the back with the rest of the stuff. I looked back over my shoulder at Ashley, who was slathering her exposed arms and legs in suntan lotion. Our eyes met and I gave a "good job" smile while Ashley returned a knowing wink. The plan was in motion.

■ ■ ■

The caravan pulled up to the riverbank, and the dust from the gravel road settled. Each of the campers climbed out one at a time and were greeted by a counselor handing out helmets and life vests.

That girl Maddy clipped her helmet on and pulled the chinstrap tight so it was snug on her head. As she did, I walked by, throwing on my own life vest.

"Have fun today," she said in my passing direction.

I turned and gave her a devious smirk. "I wouldn't worry about it." Walking away, I could tell that threw Maddy off—but then again, I have that effect on people.

A brief while later, a scream could be heard. "Hey, wait! That's my raft! Catch it!" Cahak yelled, running into the riverbank, trying to hold up his baggy trunks while chasing after his raft. Everyone stopped what they were doing immediately to help Cahak catch his fleeing raft as it went barreling down the Packer River—that is, *almost* everyone did.

I slyly backed away from the frantic mob of campers and counselors who were all hitting the water and splashing around like a bunch of goons trying to save Cahak's raft. I had about twenty-five seconds until I had to get back and pretend like I didn't nudge the raft downstream, I estimated.

I kicked up a little dust and swung my arms as I made my way to Jack's raft, my transport for the day. I flipped open Jack's knapsack with both extended index fingers and rifled through the contents: an iPod mini, a pack of smokes, and black-handled folding knife with a serrated steel blade that I, with every fiber of my consciousness absolutely, positively knew I shouldn't have taken but pocketed anyway. Returning back to the knapsack, with screams and splashing in the background as my soundtrack, I finally found what I was looking for—the phony map. It didn't even look real, I found from my critique of the forgery. I, at least, would have had some finesse with the copy, giving some sort of credit to whatever dope I was trying to fool with it.

I got off of my knees and headed over to Telly's raft, opened up her bag, finding the map inside, and swapped it with the fake. With the real map in hand, I danced my way back to Jack's open knapsack, tossed it in like a Frisbee, and flipped the bag back shut.

I stood there, arms akimbo, thinking about what I'd just done. *This should be fun*, I thought. *The prank is good . . . not great*, I continued, scrutinizing my own work. Ever the perfectionist, I am. *You do what you can with what you're given, I guess. Lesson is, if you come swinging at the king, you better make sure he isn't eavesdropping from outside of an open cabin window.*

I then found a little clearing off of the bank that was surrounded by trees leading into the river. I made my way through the trees, into the soggy sand and branches before submerging my whole body into the water so no one could hear me. I swam as far into the center of the river that I could before emerging next to the rest of the crowd pulling and tugging Cahak's raft back to shore. I pushed from the back and no one was the wiser.

Everyone was able to make it back to the beach, some collapsing, while others made sure the raft was secure.

"Well," Jack said to Telly between huffs and puffs, "we're off to a strong start this summer, eh, Captain?"

Telly looked at Jack, with both hands on her knees, still trying to catch her breath.

Back on shore, people began to relax and dry off after that mini pre-adventure to rescue the wayward raft. Telly gathered the kids together and stood before us while drops of river water dripped onto her clipboard.

"Right, now that we have all of that straightened out, let's get everyone situated with their rafts." She pointed with her pen without looking up from her clipboard, "Birch Bunk, over there. Maple Bunk, right there," she continued. "Spruce Bunk, here. Pine, you're over there." I marched to my raft to link up with the rest of my bunkmates. She pointed down to the raft below where her sneaker rested. "And Hemlock, you're with me in this one."

Everyone broke free and found their rafts for the day. Ashley helped Maddy over the side of theirs and they both sat next to each other. Telly took a handful of her own hair and wrung the water out as much as possible, then plastered on a smile. "All right, let's do this!"

Before she could get herself comfortable in the back of her raft, I could see Telly looking between her and my raft. I noticed this while I switched into a dry T-shirt before getting my life vest back on.

Something was not sitting well with her, I could sense it. She was doing math in her head and it wasn't looking good for my plan. I had to play it cool. Finally, she got out of the raft and jogged up to Jack, who was getting situated with our raft, and pulled him aside.

“Hey, I’m going to take TJ in my raft,” she ordered.

“Sure thing,” Jack complied. “What’s up?”

“I don’t know. Just a feeling, I think.”

“Well, this is your show. I’m just a guest star.”

She turned and addressed the Pines raft with a whistle between her teeth. “TJ, you’re coming with me.”

I looked up, trying to act confused. “What? Why? What the heck did I do?”

“We’re just calling it sibling time,” she replied, straight-faced. “Let’s go, hop to.”

“This is bull crap!” I protested. I knew that I couldn’t let on why I didn’t want to get into the Hemlock raft or I’d get busted. Like Telly said earlier, I’d have to stay at camp forever and become the director of this junk or whatever. “Why can’t I hang out with my friends today? I didn’t do anything!”

“Yeah, so I wasn’t really asking,” Telly demanded.

"Get up and into my raft now." She picked up my backpack and tossed it into my chest. "Let's go."

I reluctantly stood up, holding my backpack to my chest, and walked toward the Hemlock raft. I looked back over my shoulder at the Pine raft. *This could be bad*, I thought. There was no way of knowing where the girl's map would take us, if anywhere at all. *Although, this could be fun*, I assured myself. Who knew what adventure this would lead us on?

I tossed my backpack into Hemlock's raft and jumped in. I took my seat in the far back, much like the bus, next to my sister's seat. Maddy turned and saw the new member of the rafting crew, much to her dismay. I just returned the scowl and directed my attention to the river as the raft began to embark on its journey. I grabbed my oar and began to paddle. After a while I closed my eyes, feeling the sun cover my face. *Heck,* I thought, *at least we'll have a day away from the crummy old camp.*

CHAPTER 5

WE WERE A FEW MILES OUT AND OUR RAFT had already lost sight of the others. It wasn't a big deal at first, as the trip started off pleasant enough. We saw all types of rock formations and trees that were taller than a lot of buildings I had seen in the city.

Telly was doing her best to navigate us back to the others, but was also distracted with TJ using his oar to pick up water out of the river and bring it into the raft.

"Okay, I think up after this bend there should be an eddy that will allow us to stop and figure out where we went wrong," Telly said from the back, analyzing the map closer.

"Who is Eddy?" Ashley asked.

Telly dropped the map from her face and looked at Ashley. "*An* eddy. That means a place in the middle of the river where the current will stop taking our raft downstream and flow the opposite direction. It will safely stop our raft from moving so we can assess what to do next."

Telly brought the map back up to her eyes and said under her breath, "Where in the hell are we? None of this looks familiar . . . "

The raft drifted tranquilly down the river; the only noise came from the water itself. We passed the bend, and sure enough there was no eddy in sight. Only what looked like a stronger current pulling us faster downstream.

I wrapped the hoopi, the rope within the raft, around my finger and then unwound it. I then wrapped it around my wrist while I observed the surroundings—the swaying branches over the river, the rocks that had shifted and cracked over thousands of years. One boulder looked just like a caribou. Another looked just like George Clooney.

■ ■ ■

I pulled up my oar and placed it on the floor of the raft, stretched out my legs, and let nature do its thing. There could have been worse ways to spend the day, even being trapped in a raft with Maddy and Telly, so I didn't really sweat it. I would have dozed off right there, too, if I hadn't heard a strange creak in the trees. Opening one eye, I caught the sight of something I had only seen in fifth-grade science class—a pulley of some sort drilled into the outstretched tree branch.

I sat up and followed the sound from one side of the river to the other, where I spotted another pulley on a thick tree branch. The one I was looking at, however, was anchored by a black, rusted barrel slowly moving from the top of the branch to the ground.

“What the hell?” I heard myself asking, not sure what it was I was seeing. But at the exact moment the question mark floated out of my curious mouth, the barrel plummeted out of the tree, hitting the ground with incredible force, which tightened the wire strung between the riverbanks and forced the front of our raft to flip high into the air.

It’s strange how fast it happened, really. One second everyone was riding in the Hemlock raft, peacefully enjoying the trip. The next second, most of us sailed through the air, able to see the water far below us. Then suddenly we were submerged under the thunderous current of the Packer River.

Telly wasn’t the first to emerge from below the water, but she was the first to speak rather than scream. “Is everyone okay?!” She got nothing back in response other than cries and frantic splashing.

My upper body burst through the water as I wiped the water from my eyes and coughed the rest out of my mouth. “Telly? Telly, what’s going on?” I looked up above us and saw the tight wire that had flipped our raft. That was planned. That was a trap.

"I don't know, I don't know," she barked, trying to stay calm, but the nerves had taken over. "What is that noise?"

Telly and I looked downstream in tandem to see that the water was no longer moving forward in one continual stream—no, it was falling directly off of a cliff.

Telly's eyes widened. "SWIM TO THE SHORE!"

It was either from the pure shock and confusion of going airborne in the middle of a body of water or it was plain, natural teenage gut instinct, but nobody listened to her. Each of the campers were spastically splashing, trying their hardest to swim anywhere *but* the shore.

A lot of the rafters eventually found safety. Some held onto tree branches, others crawled onto the sand. Telly made her way over to two campers who were floundering in the river. She dove under the water and then grabbed both around their collarbones, kicking her way back to the shallow part of the river.

I got myself out, breathing heavily in and out on the slippery rocks of the riverbed, when I noticed that not everyone was there. I waved my hands in the air to catch Telly's attention from across the river.

"Not everyone is here!" I said, not giving her a chance to respond. Looking at the overturned raft a few hundred feet from the waterfall, I knew exactly where Maddy was.

I dove in, and I let the current push me as I swam faster and harder to the raft.

"TJ, GET BACK HERE!" I could hear Telly scream from upstream.

I grabbed onto the overturned raft and found the flip line, the rope attached to the middle of the raft, and used it as a guide below the water. Everything went silent as I searched for her under the raft and eventually got to her. Under the raft, but above the water, I was able to take a breath of air.

"I can't get loose!" Maddy said, with both hands above her head on the floor of the raft.

I saw the rope she was playing with wrapped around her neck, winding all the way down to her ankle. "Okay, I'm going back out, and I'm going to use the flip line to get the raft back upright. I need you to hug this bench as hard as you can so you'll be in the boat when it flips. I'm going to pound on the outside to let you know when we're good to go. We can cut you loose once we're both back in the raft."

"Okay," she responded without hesitation.

I went back under and hung onto the flip line, emerging from the water back to the chaos. I pulled my body to the top of the raft and collapsed for a second. The swimming and the climbing had knocked the breath straight out of me. The waterfall was approaching fast, which left me no choice but to find the D ring and tie the flip line to it. Once the deed was done, I pushed myself to my knees, pounded on the raft to let Maddy know she was about to travel, and stood all of the way up on the flipped raft.

I leapt off the boat, which made the slack rope taut and turned the raft upright. I grabbed onto the side and pulled myself up and over into it. Maddy was up, and she tried to untangle herself from the rope while I pulled the knife from my pocket.

"You have to get this off of me," Maddy cried in a panic.

"I'm trying," my voice broke while I sawed through the thickly wound-up cord. The handle of the knife was too slick from the water, and so it slipped right out of out of my hand.

We both watched in horror as the knife bounced from its handle to its blade, somersaulted back to the handle, then finally stuck the landing with the blade buried deep, which popped the polyurethane floor of the raft.

"Ah . . . " I muttered, fresh out of descriptors in my vocabulary.

The lip of the raft went over the edge of the waterfall, like the beginning of a rollercoaster. And there were no more options. We couldn't jump overboard.

We wouldn't have been able to avoid the jagged rocks, which surrounded us.

The only thing Maddy could say as we were greeted with the sight of the hundred-foot drop that could possibly be our end was, "*Hang on*!"

■ ■ ■

"Stay here!" I ordered the two crying campers I had just brought to shore.

"Telly! Telly! Don't leave us, please!" Emily wept.

"It's okay, it's okay. You have to stay here. I have to go get TJ and Maddy, okay?"

I ran along the shore to the booming waterfall and climbed on top of the jagged rocks to get a better view. I couldn't see through the dense water falling and the mist that it generated. I climbed off of the rocks and worked my way through the forest to find a way down below, but it was hopeless. The land ended where the waterfall began.

It'd be at least a half day's trip to get down there,

I realized. With the seven remaining campers, I couldn't possibly endanger them anymore by keeping them, unprepared, in the middle of the woods through the night. The only option was to lead those kids back to camp, where they would be safe and taken care of. There, I would gather a search party.

CHAPTER 6

"TJ, are you there?" I tried to speak these words, but something was keeping me from breathing. Everything but my nose was underwater, as I was shuttled downriver by the deflated piece of plastic that was once the Hemlock cabin's raft. I thrashed around for a second, bringing myself above the water to breathe. I was able to unsnarl myself from the flattened raft and then hung onto the side for support.

I looked around, bobbing up and down in the river. The waterfall was no longer in sight, although I could still hear it far behind me. The current wasn't as strong as it was before, and it lazily guided me forward. On both sides of the river, there were thick walls of trees as far as I could see. The rope remained snug around my ankle as I kicked downstream.

A few yards forward, I noticed something that could have very well been a log just off to the side of the river. A log with legs being swept gently back and forth by the slow current.

"TJ?" I asked aloud, as I kicked harder towards him.

I made it onto the shore but I fell backwards, as I was anchored by the raft still in the river. I used my free leg to pull myself backwards and got the deflated mess onto shore. I untangled the rope from around my ankle and flipped TJ over onto his back.

"TJ?" I asked again, as I noticed that his lips were a light color of blue. He wasn't moving at all, including his chest, which should have been bringing air in and out of his body. "TJ?!"

I pushed his head back and breathed into his mouth as I watched his chest rise. I removed my mouth from his and watched as his chest fell. I then began to push on his chest, one pump after another to the tune of myself softly, but fearfully, singing, "Ah, ah, ah, ah, stayin' alive. Stayin' alive."

Nothing. I breathed into him again, as his chest rose and then fell.

"Stayin' alive. Stayin' alive."

Rise, fall. Rise, fall.

"Stay alive," I desperately pleaded under my breath, "please . . . "

Then, as if he were answering my wish, river water shot out of TJ's mouth like a human water fountain, which hit me directly in the face.

Before TJ coughed up more water, I heard him say something in a daze, like "Dad, no!" He then turned over on his side to get it all out. He breathed heavily and heaved while he closed his eyes. He rolled on to his back, with one hand resting on his chest, the other over his forehead.

He removed one arm from over his face and finally opened his eyes to see me hovering over him. In shock, he pushed me backward by my shoulders and crawled away toward the riverbank. "*Get the hell off of me*!" he demanded in a panic. His eyes darted manically around at the forest. "Where . . . ?" he questioned. "How . . . ?" The water, the wind, and the breathing were the only sounds that were made while I watched in shock as this person came back to life before my very eyes.

His breathing slowed down slightly. "What was that?" he asked. "You had the sausage links this morning at breakfast?"

I picked up a short stick and threw it at TJ's chest. He chuckled to himself and wiped his hand through his hair as he observed the environment.

"So, we can check barreling down a waterfall off of the bucket list, I guess," he said as he picked himself up off of the ground. "How did you . . . ?" he said, as he pointed to his own chest. "Where did you learn that?"

I got up and brushed the dirt and leaves off of me. "The YMCA. My brother Jacob almost died when I was ten by choking on a piece of hot dog. I couldn't do anything and it made me feel really helpless. Fortunately, the teenager working behind the counter knew the Heimlich maneuver and saved him in the middle of the restaurant."

"That was lucky," TJ responded.

"It sure was. But not so much for Jacob," I replied.

"Why?"

"Have you ever been saved by a teenager wearing a hot dog costume in the middle of a crowded restaurant?"

"Good point." TJ looked around and saw the flattened raft resting on the shore. "This ours?"

"Yes."

TJ flipped the plastic over and investigated it thoroughly. He finally found the handle of the knife and pulled the blade out of the raft. He closed it shut and pocketed it in his jeans.

"Okay, from the sound of it, we're not too far from the waterfall," he said as he unbuckled his life vest and dropped it on the ground. "But that was a straight drop so there's no way to get back up it.

Meaning we need to follow this river the opposite direction, going north, if we want to find a road at all."

"Will we make it to one before nightfall?" I wondered aloud.

"I don't suppose you have your phone on you?" TJ optimistically asked.

"I've never owned one. Plus, it says specifically in the camp manual that we weren't supposed to bring them up to Dream Haven at all or they'd be confiscated."

"Okay, okay. You don't have one," TJ sighed as he pulled out his smashed and cracked phone from his soggy jean pocket and let the river water pour out of it. "Getting bars out here wouldn't be an option anyways." He thought for a second after he tossed the phone aside. "Well, actually there's one way to do this," TJ said as he stepped back and looked up into the sky.

He stretched his right arm out, with his hand pointed sideways, as if he was blocking out the sun.

Then he stretched his left arm out and put that hand below his right. He stared up at the sun, and he did some math in his head.

"Well, we have about two hours of sunlight left. Then it'll be dark, and that ain't gonna do us any favors navigating through the forest."

"So what do we do?"

He took a breath and weighed out his options. "Well, like I said, we follow the river as far as we can. But eventually we'll have to find or make some sort of shelter." He picked up a long stick and broke it over his knee. "This is Mother Nature's house and we invited ourselves in. And she doesn't like unannounced visitors." He handed over one half of the stick to me. "We gotta play by her rules. And those are the rules of three."

"What is that?" I asked as I held the stick sideways.

"You can only live three hours without shelter, three days without water, and three weeks without food."

I stabbed into the ground with my stick. "Then we better get moving."

■ ■ ■

We forged our way through the forest and dragged the raft behind us by the flip line while we took our lead from the slow-moving Packer River. The heat wrapped the two of us up like a warm fleece blanket right out of the dryer—making sure we knew that it was there.

"What is that?" I asked after I dropped my part of the flip line and pointed forward.

We got closer and found Maddy's backpack along with many other backpacks from the raft scattered along the shore.

"Oh God. This is amazing!" Maddy said as she picked up her bag and examined it. She unzipped it fully and did an inventory of everything within the pack. "They must have all drifted past me from the waterfall!"

"I don't suppose you have some tacos in there, do you?" I asked and peered into the open bag.

"No, but I have all of the medicine I need to take today. I'm almost out of spoons and things would have gotten bad."

"Spoons?" I asked, confused.

"People with my condition go by the twelve-spoon rule. When you run out of your spoons for the day, things get bad," Maddy answered, as quickly as a reflex.

"How bad?"

Maddy lowered the bag and looked at the ground for a second. "You don't have to see it, anyways, I have what I need. So don't worry about it."

I threw my hands in the air. "Don't think that I am! I just wanted to know what I'd have to deal with if you didn't have it. Like, if you'd turn into a werewolf or something."

Maddy pulled out a pair of jeans, her faded gray and pink hoodie, and sneakers from the bag, then unclipped her vest and tossed it aside. She slipped the jeans on over her swimsuit and threw the hoodie on.

I looked up from one of the backpacks I was rummaging through. “Nothing but girls’ clothes in these bags. I feel like I’m in freaking Forever 21.” I tossed the backpack aside and watched as Maddy zipped up her hoodie. “I don’t know how you can wear that thing. It has to be ninety degrees right now,” I observed.

“This thing is comfortable in any temperature,” she rebutted while she tied the pink laces of her dirty sneakers. She stood up after her full wardrobe change and threw the backpack over her shoulder. “Well?” she asked. “Shall we?”

The sun slowly hid itself behind the horizon, letting us unwilling hikers know, “You don’t have to go home, but you can’t stay here.” A storm was coming.

We pulled to a stop as the sun gave its final wave and collapsed into the ground. Our clothes were soggy with sweat, and the mosquitos had already begun lining up for the blood buffet. The rumble of thunder could be heard in the distance.

"Shelter and water. Those are the top of our to-do list," I said through the exhaustion.

"What are we going to do for those two?" Maddy asked, perched forward from the weight of her backpack. "My throat is so dry I can actually feel the full words I say as they come out."

"The river water is out. Can't drink that stuff, too much risk," I explained before I looked below me at the raft. "But I think I have a way around that."

Maddy stood up and dropped her backpack. "What do you need me to do?"

I pulled out the knife from my pocket and released the blade from the handle. "I need you to find sticks. Long, sturdy sticks. As many as you can. We can start building something for a shelter with those."

"Can do," Maddy said before she began her hunt.

I bent down and began to examine the raft, looking for the attached polyurethane pouch sewn into the body. Once I found it, I pulled it taut and sawed along the straight line. I released the pouch from the raft. It was the size and shape of a purse. I held it up and examined my handiwork. A little crude on the sides, but it would still work. I picked up the flip line, took just about a foot of it, and cut it free from the rest.

I closed the knife and replaced it in my jean pocket, picked up my new materials, and began marching. I didn't have to go far before I stumbled across what I was looking for: a chinquapin oak tree. I threw the piece of flip line and raft around my shoulders and began climbing. Once I reached the sturdiest branch, I threw my legs around it like I was mounting a horse.

I found the biggest, widest group of leaves that hung from the branch and wrapped the piece of plastic around them like I would a birthday present—making sure there was enough open room at the bottom. It held the raft in place, and I tied it to the bundled stems of leaves with the piece of flip line, which secured the two together.

I hugged the branch, and I let my body roll off so I hung a few feet from the ground. I let go and fell to the ground, where I looked up at my work. That should do the trick, I thought to myself. I had only seen it done once, but we really had no other options at that point. Rain clouds began to form over the forest, the distant sound of thunder became a cautionary cry for what was about to come.

I walked back to the raft—the rendezvous for us displaced campers—before I heard my name being called.

"TJ!" Maddy said from not too far away. "I think we're set!"

I followed her voice and met Maddy, who stood before an incredibly large uprooted tree.

"This is perfect!" I excitedly reacted. "Here, hold on a second," I ordered before I ran back to the raft. The clock was ticking, and sooner than later the storm was going to hit us. So I dragged the flattened boat over to the uprooted tree and draped it over the exposed roots, which dangled over the deep hole within the ground like spindly witch fingers.

Together Maddy and I secured the plastic to the roots. Going down the line, I cut into the raft while Maddy threaded the flip line around each stem. Right when the first drop of rain landed on Maddy's forehead, our home for the night was complete. We both ducked under the new roof and burrowed into the earth. Maddy used her backpack as a cushion while I got cozy on a pile of leaves and bush I had gathered.

We watched the dark sky slowly take over the view, and then the rain began to pour. As we sat there, protected from at least the weather for now, we gave ourselves the gift of relaxation for the moment.

"If we had an iPad right now, I'd say this would be better than being at camp," I said without a look over at my new roommate.

Maddy yearningly sighed. "I could go for a fire. Maybe some s'mores—I dunno. If we were talking about what would make our new digs perfect."

"Find me something that isn't soaked from the

rain and maybe I can get part of that wish fulfilled for you."

Maddy thought for a second. "Actually . . . " she started as she sat up and brought her backpack to her lap. She unzipped the bag and blindly rooted around in it; eventually she found what she was looking for. She triumphantly held it up in front of my face: a tube of cherry lip balm.

I looked at it, confused for a second. "I don't think my lips are that cracked," I said, slightly touching my mouth.

"No, dummy, you've never done this before?" Maddy asked as she uncapped the tube. She gave the bottom a few turns and revealed a half inch of the lip balm. She pinched it between her index finger and thumb, and then rolled it into a little ball.

"Can you give me a spark?"

"I can give it a shot," I complied and pulled the pocketknife out of my jeans.

I searched for a dry stone in the ground and found one buried in the earth. Maddy placed the balled-up wax on a dead leaf between the two of us and sat back. I dug the rock out, wiped the dirt off of it on the leg of my jeans, struck the blade across it, and it garnered sparks immediately.

"Try to hit it right on the lip balm," Maddy instructed. "This is usually easier with a lighter . . . "

I struck the stone a few more times; each one got closer to the ball of wax. Finally, a lone spark met the lip balm, which made a small ball of fire in the middle of the dead leaf.

"Whoa!" I exclaimed. I sat back on my knees and watched the magic show unfold in front of us.

Maddy got closer to the burning leaf and warmed her hands over the miniature makeshift bonfire. "My brothers and their friends used to do this at family barbecues all of the time. They'd roll up a dozen of these and throw them through fire pits at each other, like flaming bullets." She half chuckled. "Idiots."

We watched in amazement as the flaming ball of lip relief burned bright and warm—all while the pitter patter of rain drummed on the plastic rooftop of our new shelter. As the glowing ball began to grow dim, our depleted energy began to show in our heavy eyes. Slowly, one blink after the next, both of our eyes were finally at rest for the first time in the day.

■ ■ ■

I burst through the double doors of Dream Haven, soaked head to toe and shivering.

"Oh my God, Telly!" Venkman proclaimed from across the rec room. "You never came back! We were so worried . . . "

"Are they here?" I demanded, panicked. "Where are they?"

"Who?!" Venkman asked.

"TJ and Maddy," I answered as I glided across the room toward the camp director. "I—I lost them. The waterfall . . . "

"Waterfall?" Venkman did the math. "Where is the rest of your bunk? Are they safe?"

"I got them all back. They are in their bunk,

terrified as all hell, but they are safe." I fell into a chair next to a board set up for checkers. "It was a fake map. It was probably TJ, but it led us down the wrong route. Our raft flipped, and TJ and Maddy went over the waterfall with it."

"Oh my God," Venkman sighed to himself.

I looked up. "I know where they are. We have to get back out there and save them."

"Telly, look at it outside. It's like the storm of the century right now. It's hailing for Pete's sake." Venkman protested.

"I know what's going on outside. I just hiked six miles through the forest in the pitch-black darkness with ten sobbing campers. And if I have to do it again tonight by myself, then so be it."

"You're not going anywhere," Venkman ordered me.

"Two of your campers, one of whom is disabled and the other is my baby brother, are out there alone. We have to do something! Call a search party!"

Venkman sighed. "The storm knocked out the

phone line an hour ago. And there is no cell phone service up here."

"Where's the bus?" I asked as I stood up from the chair.

"Cahak took it into town to grab the supplies Buzz asked for yesterday. I'm guessing he's trapped there until the storm ends."

I let out a long, exasperated sigh and walked toward the window. As I looked out at the great, dark unknown, lightning cracked and showed nothing but endless trees going as far as I could see. TJ and Maddy were out there, somewhere. And all I could do at that very moment was wait.

CHAPTER 7

I DIDN'T KNOW WHAT TIME IT WAS—THAT WAS the first thing I thought of after opening my eyes. The storm had picked up while we slept, with the lightning cracking hard. The light was so dazzling, it illuminated the entire moonless night sky, which made it feel like it was bright and early in the day.

I stretched my back and readjusted the backpack behind me like a worn pillow. TJ was out for the count and his snores reminded me of my dog Dexter. Dexter had a deviated septum, which messed up his breathing while he slept. I always thought it was hilarious to hear him snore on nights when it was hard for me to fall asleep. I'd lay in bed and listen to my pup whistle some tunes in his slumber, and that would eventually help me fall into mine. It was like those white noise machines—the ones that play the sound of waves in the ocean crashing onto a beach, or the tick of a grandfather clock.

I watched TJ snore in and out, wondering if he had a deviated septum. If so, should he have it checked out? Pondering this, I removed the faded gray and pink sweater from under me and draped it over my torso like a blanket. Finally, I warmed up and I made my final adjustments to go back to sleep—when I saw it.

The brief punctuation of light had shown something peeking from around the tree away in the distance. Slowly, I sat up and let the sweater drop off of me. Lightning cracked, and there it was. I couldn't concretely say at that moment that what I saw was a "him"—or "her" for that matter. What I saw was something of a shape. Something I knew was there, lurking, its eyes piercing me even from afar.

I turned and nervously nudged TJ.

"TJ," I whispered, "TJ, you have to wake up . . . "

TJ snorted, coughed, then resumed snoring. I nudged his body harder with my shoulder.

"TJ, there's someone out there . . . " my whisper became more desperate.

"Wha—I'm up, ma!" TJ yelled with his eyes shut.

Without wasting any more time, I found TJ's knife between us and flipped it open. I turned back to the uprooted tree's entrance, knife outstretched, ready to fight. When the lightning cracked again, the shape was gone. The tree was its normal shape, nothing was out of the ordinary.

My breathing stayed fast and staggered as I held the outstretched knife, looking around to make sure the shape was indeed nowhere in sight. I made a plan to stay awake and be on lookout for the rest of the night.

■ ■ ■

"Morning, sunshine!"

I was the first thing Maddy saw when she opened her eyes. She looked down and saw that she still had the knife open and held up close against her chest.

"Had some nightmares, did we?"

"I, uh . . . " she said dreamily and mulled over my question. Maddy closed the knife and handed it back to me.

I took it and placed it back in my jean pocket. "Here, I want to show you something."

We crawled out from the shelter and into the bright, early morning light. The storm had done a pretty good job redecorating the joint and had left a harsh, humid wake behind. I marched ahead as Maddy zipped up her hoodie and got her bearings back.

"I thought I saw something last night," she said.

"I'm sure you did. You're in a dark, strange place. Your mind is bound to play tricks on you," I dismissed her easily.

"No—it wasn't that. I . . . " she trailed off. "I know I saw something . . . someone."

"Well I'm glad you didn't invite them in for tea or anything. Our one-bedroom was cramped as is," I said before I stopped and pointed up. "Check this out."

I climbed up the tree again, untied the flip line, and cradled the full piece of raft down to Maddy. I watched her face when she opened the makeshift satchel in her hands.

"You asked for water, you get some water," I said as I crossed my arms, satisfied.

Maddy took a long, serious gulp and let some water go down the side of her face onto her hoodie. She let out a contented sigh.

"How did you do this?" she asked before she took another tug.

"If your body wears any plastic, it's bound to sweat a lot more than usual, right? Same deal with these leaves. You wrap 'em up, not letting them get enough air, they begin to sweat a lot faster. Hence, the water you have right there."

Maddy lowered the bag and let out a gasp of air from not breathing. "How often are you wrapping yourself in plastic?" She passed the satchel to me. "And why didn't you just collect rainwater from the storm last night?"

Before I brought the plastic up to my lips, I thought about her question. "I don't know. I guess I've always done things in life the more complicated way." Then I took a long, satisfying pull of the leaves' sweat, closed the pouch, and secured it with the piece of flip line. I wiped my mouth with the back of my hand.

"Come on," I said and dropped our new water bottle into her backpack. "I've got something else to show you that I found this morning."

■ ■ ■

We hiked through the forest as TJ followed the line of destruction that the storm produced and I trailed behind him, stepping under overturned trees.

After a while of silence, I finally asked, "Did your grandfather really teach you this?" I walked and held both straps of my backpack. "I mean, everything. What we're doing out here to survive."

TJ continued to walk along and thought about my question before answering. Which was strange. So far as I knew him, he never really felt the need to think about what he was going to say before actually saying it.

"Yeah, I guess he did. He wanted his culture to be passed down no matter what. My dad was never interested in it. He basically skipped it so I guess we were grandpa's last chance."

"Your dad never learned?"

"He had no time. He was in the business of saving lives himself. He was a fireman, so he was never really around to begin with."

I kept my eyes to the ground. "I see."

"They'd ship me off to my grandpa every summer," TJ continued. "We'd spend whole weeks out in the woods, learning about reading the Earth and how to use it resourcefully and stuff. They said it was for my own good. That I'd learn about who I really was. When my grandpa died last year, they had nothing else to distract me with. So they forced me to come up here this summer."

"Distract you?" I asked curiously.

"I mean," TJ backpedaled, "I tend to get myself into problems that are usually pretty easy to avoid. I guess I just like excitement a little too much."

"What kind of problems?"

"Nothing serious, I think it's usually misunderstandings."

"Like what? Like what happened with your dad?" I train-brained.

TJ fully stopped and left me to walk a few paces before I realized I was walking alone. I stopped and turned around, realizing what had just happened.

"I'm sorry, I uh . . . " I tried to get out.

TJ's face was a stone block. Emotion may have been trying to break through it, but he was using all of his force to make sure that it didn't.

"And what do you know about my dad, huh?" he said as heat rose in his voice. "What the hell do you know about him?"

"Nothing, I . . . "

"You think I killed him? That's it, right? You think he's dead and it's because of me." His face was red-hot.

"No, I don't know anything . . . "

"That's right, you don't. If you weren't wrapped up like some idiot under that raft, we wouldn't even be in this mess. And since I'm the only one out here that knows anything useful, I'm the only chance of getting your crippled self out of these woods alive!"

I stood there, letting the words hit me when I knew that I shouldn't have. Arguing wasn't going to get us to safety any sooner, so I accepted it—it was nothing I hadn't heard before. So I turned around and started walking away, before I stopped myself.

"You know what? No," I exclaimed, turning back around. "You don't get to do that. You don't get to push your guilt or insecurities onto me. I deal with enough of that bull crap every single day, and I'm sure as hell not adding anymore to my already full plate, especially from someone like you."

"Oh, someone like me? Who is that, huh?" TJ asked, both hands on his hips.

I began to say something but stopped myself. All I could do was let out an angry sigh. "I don't get it. I really don't. It's like you go extra out of your way to act like a total jerk to anyone who is in your wake. Why? You seem smart and some people actually respect you. What the hell are you trying to protect yourself from?"

TJ stood there and looked right through me with anger in his eyes. He broke the silence and moved towards me. "Whatever. We have to keep moving," he demanded and knocked into my shoulder.

We walked in silence for a bit and let the tension build, along with the heat of the sun, when TJ finally stopped and pointed.

"There," he said quietly. Before us was an old log cabin. The skeleton of it, really, as it had been severely burned down to the ground. All that was left was the floor, the chimney, and the steps that lead up to it. "I haven't scouted it thoroughly yet. I got up at sunrise to scout out our area and make a game plan. I wanted to get you first thing when I stumbled across it."

We walked up to the charred remains of the cabin.

"You stay here for a second. I'm gonna pop in, see if anyone is home," TJ said and climbed the stairs.

I didn't respond verbally, I just nodded and waited for him to be out of sight. I stood there and contemplatively looked around me at nature. I heard the birds sing their summer camp songs. I saw the sun break through the wall of green leaves. It was peaceful and horrifying at the exact same time—to be so small in such a big place.

▪ ▪ ▪

I stepped down the three burned steps that remained from the destroyed cabin and spun a beaten-up tin can in my palm.

“This was all I could find, which is something at least,” I said and handed it over to Maddy. “Not sure what it is—and I didn’t find a can opener.”

I bent down and picked through leaves and debris, while Maddy turned the can over in her crinkled hands and examined it.

“It could be anything for all I care, we haven’t eaten in awhile. Do you see any rocks with edges?” I asked, “Maybe I can beat it open.”

Maddy stopped turning the can and surveyed the area. “I don’t think that’ll be necessary,” she said and walked over to a slab of concrete near the cabin. She got down on both knees, placed the can upside down on the slab, and then began to scrape it back and forth as hard she could.

“I always wondered what it would’ve been like to be an only child,” she mused, while she scraped the can across the concrete. “You know, to be the center of someone’s attention for once.”

“You’ve got a captive audience right in front of you,” I smirked.

She scrubbed the can. "That's not what I mean. I'm the youngest of six," she half-chuckled. "People thought we were Mormon."

She scraped faster. "When there's that many bodies in a house, you just become another roommate. Another mouth to feed. Which wasn't too often for me. Being the youngest also meant being the last in line for dinner. So whatever was left was mine."

She continued to rub, back and forth, back and forth, and never broke her concentration.

"One time my dad was between jobs, which is a funny saying because he was never really between jobs. He would pick up what was thrown at him." She stopped to take in a breath then started to scrape again.

"It got so bad that all we had to eat were potatoes that the church brought over. Every night, mom would boil them and serve what she could. Until one night my dad came home, no job in hand. Something just . . . snapped. Shoves were exchanged, and eventually my mom . . . was on the ground. He pushed the pot of boiling water on top of her." There she stopped moving the can, stood up, and walked over to me.

"It was then that I promised that I would never let hunger get the best of me or anyone around me again," she said and tossed the can into my hands. I examined it, noticing that the top ridge had been ground down to the lid. I held it in one hand, and I used the other to push it open with my thumb.

"You'd be surprised what you learn when you're hungry enough," Maddy said, after she pushed a piece of hair out of her eyes.

"I, uh . . . " I mumbled while looking at the now-opened can. What was left of the label had what looked like a bean with a mustache and sombrero on. After a few seconds, I offered the can to Maddy. "Here," I said with my outstretched arm, "to the founder of the feast."

Maddy grabbed it from me, cradling it in her elbow and taking a scoop of brown lumps out of the can with two fingers. It looked like it was the greatest thing she had ever tasted.

"Plus I wanted you to test it so we knew it wasn't dog food," I said with a smile.

That made Maddy laugh, with bits of refried beans coming out of her mouth. I had never seen her smile before that moment—at least, I was never the cause of her smiling.

"Hey, at least it's not potatoes," she joked, and we both laughed.

The moment was interrupted when the snap of a branch came from a few yards behind us.

CHAPTER 8

"Shh . . . " TJ nervously whispered. "What was that?"

"I don't know," I said and lowered the can.

"It came from over there," TJ pointed.

We both crept through the woods and tracked what sounded like someone or something not too far ahead of us.

"What if it's a bear?" I asked.

"No way, not up here," TJ answered.

"What if it's something that doesn't want us here?"

"What if it's help?" TJ responded with his own

question. "All we can do is hang back and make sure nothing or no one has the jump on us."

We followed the sound, attempting to keep our distance.

"Do you know where they are going?" I whispered to TJ.

"I'm trying my best to track them, and I think we have their trail," he replied and pointed to the ground ahead of us as we moved forward. "They're coming from somewhere sandy."

"How can you tell?"

"When you walk uphill, you dig your foot into the ground more, see?" TJ addressed the footprints dug deep into the hill we were climbing. "They've brought sand back with them from wherever they were. You can also see rocks that have been pushed into the earth by a large boot. And even broken twigs, see?"

"I do," I answered.

"They have a destination in mind and they're trying to get to it. Fast."

We reached the top of the hill and saw a figure,

a man wearing a plaid shirt and orange vest, a few hundred yards ahead of us.

"That's our guy," TJ said and knelt down behind a log, so we could gain a bit more distance from our guy in orange. "We need to see where he's going and scope it out before we know it's safe. Best case scenario, it's our way out of here."

"And worst case scenario?" I asked as I took a knee next to him.

TJ just looked at me with the type of eyes that said, *Your idea is just as good as mine.* He looked forward. "Okay, let's go."

With stealth, we made our way through the acres of forest, from one tree to the next, and closed in on our prey. The farther in we went, the clearer an opening in the forest became—like a bright light at the end of a very long tunnel.

TJ took a brief peek from behind a tree, went back, then slowly revealed himself from cover.

"Wait a second . . . " TJ said.

"What is it?" I asked as I stepped away from my tree.

"This is a rock quarry!"

We walked towards the clearing more openly and were hopeful that this was our ticket back home.

"My sister was talking about this place!" TJ continued. "Meaning we're only about fifteen miles from camp."

We broached the tree line and stepped out into the glaring sun, which reflected off of the brilliant white walls of rock in front of us. The light was blinding and magnificent at the same time. A small, crystal blue lake and dirty white sand separated us two kids and the great enclosure.

"Well, here's where the sand came from. So our guy works here," TJ investigated. "Now we just need to find him."

I shielded my eyes and scanned the area. I saw the man we were tracking across the way as he stepped into a trailer. "There!" I pointed out enthusiastically.

We waved our arms and began to shout, and tried

our hardest to gain his attention. Unfortunately, due to distance and lack of acoustics in the venue, neither of our voices were heard. The only response we received after a few seconds was a high-pitched squeal from a PA system being turned on.

"*Three,*" the droning voice boomed out of unseen speakers.

"Oh God," TJ said wide-eyed.

"What?"

"*Two.*"

"Run," TJ demanded as he turned around and grabbed tightly onto my forearm.

"What?!"

"*One.*"

"RUN!"

The sound was loud—like a thick textbook being knocked off of a desk times a million. For a few seconds nothing happened—that is, until a giant wall of crystal blue water mightily rose from the quarry and headed straight for the forest.

TJ and I stuck together as long as we could as we

dodged trees, logs, and rocks. The water chased us ceaselessly, knocked dead trees over, and ripped up the ground from under it. We split up and tried our best to keep ahead of it. I could feel the wall taunt me as it spit on my shoulders and neck.

Small rocks began to rip through trees and leaves as they hit the ground in front of us like bullets from a machine gun. TJ covered his head with both of his arms locked behind it. He followed the gully to the right of him. The "*clack, clack, clack*" of rocks as they demolished wood deafened us.

I saw the hill in front of me, so I made it my mission to slide down it before the water threw me off of it. I looked to my right and saw TJ keeping pace, arms raised over his head. Our eyes met for a brief moment, and TJ's seemed to be pleading with me to offer him some shred of hope that we'd get out of this alive.

A burst of blood came out of TJ's left thigh first as if he was shot from behind, which took him down to one knee. He let out a pained scream and grasped at his leg. Another stream of blood came from TJ's head, which knocked his limp body down the gully.

"Oh my God!" I screamed before I lost my footing and tumbled down the hill we had climbed up. I tossed, turned, and flipped all of the way to the bottom, close to our original campsite with the raft. I dizzily crawled, then stood up and watched the water first trickle, then erupt over the edge of the hill.

I stripped off my soggy, faded pink-and-gray sweater and dropped it to the ground. I tore at the flip line attached to the roots and deflated raft with my teeth. I wrapped whatever I got loose over my body and bent down to my knees—in hopes that the wall of water would rush over me like I was a stone.

The tide instead picked me up and tossed me far down the forest. I held on to the raft as hard as I could; I received a breath here and near-suffocation there. My body was tossed around like a single sock in a washing machine on the heavy cycle.

The water began to thin out and eventually made its way to the river, after it slowly spun me to a stop in some brush. I lay on my back, cradled in the raft, and took in as much air as possible. I felt the sting in my nostrils and throat from all of the water that had surged into it.

I wiped water out of my eyes as my breath steadied, and stared up at the tops of the trees. I watched as water dripped off of the leaves.

An unknown face came into center frame of my vision. He was older, mid-to-late-thirties, but would pass off for younger if it weren't for the stress around and in his eyes. He had a handsome, rugged face with short pitch-black hair sprinkled white throughout like some sort of solar system. One of his eyes scanned me, evaluating what he had stumbled across, while the other stayed perfectly still, focused on my forehead.

I rolled away and crawled backwards on my elbows, as I wanted to put distance between the stranger and me.

He dropped the wooden crate he carried and put up one hand while he stayed where he was. "It's okay, it's okay!" he pled. "I saw it. I saw it all happen. The explosion, the—the water. You survived," he trailed for a second between breaths. "I mean—I just wanted to make sure you survived."

My breath slowed down as I looked over the stranger, my eyes going from frightened to questioning.

"You're him," I realized. "You're the one from last night. In the storm." I pushed myself up to my elbows. "You were watching us."

A small smile grew on his face. "Well, I wouldn't say I was watching," he walked a little closer. "More like observing."

He reached out a hand to offer me. I looked at it but didn't move. "From where I'm sitting, there doesn't seem to be a whole lotta difference between the two," I said to his hand.

He retracted his hand and wiped it against his clean navy blue and red North Face zip-up. "If there was anything out of the ordinary that just happened to pop up in your home overnight, you'd want to observe it, too, wouldn't you?"

"Your home?" I asked, staying put.

He stepped back so I could see him clearly. He was put together, that's for sure. Spotless brown Patagonia hiking pants matching unmarked Sorel brown leather boots. He was lean, but looked like he could take down more than double his weight. "This land, all of this land speaks to me. I've known certain trees here longer than you've been alive. Whatever this place has to offer, it offers to me so I can truly live." He looked down at me. "They're family. The trees, the birds, the squirrels—heck, even that forest tent caterpillar crawling on your hand there," he said, pointing to my left hand.

I gave a little yelp and catapulted the caterpillar through the air. The stranger laughed, turned his back to me, then back around.

"My family, they're all here. And wherever your family is—forest, neighborhood or sewer, you can bet your bottom dollar that you can call it home."

"So, uh—" I said as I started to understand. "So if

the forest speaks directly to you, then who does that make you, anyway?"

The stranger smiled wide and opened his arms. "I'm sorry, I haven't introduced myself. My name is Edgar. Edgar Hugo. And this," he said, sweeping his opened hands throughout the forest, "is my home. Now, who might you be?"

■ ■ ■

I watched the sun rise behind the storm clouds from the top floor of Dream Haven. A low rumble shook the glass, which caused me to think about something other than TJ and Maddy for a brief moment.

"What was that?" I asked as I turned my head away from the window toward the seated Venkman and Jack.

"Hmm?" Venkman let out while he bit at a hangnail on his ring finger. "Did you ask me something, Telly?"

"The building just rattled."

Venkman pulled his finger from his mouth and spat out the piece of skin. "I didn't feel anything."

I stepped away from the window and walked toward the door. "We have to get moving. We're losing time."

Venkman stood up and followed her. "But Cahak isn't back with the bus yet."

"I have to head towards the waterfall. If I know TJ, he's not just going to sit around waiting for the cavalry to show up. So we're going to have to overshoot it by a few miles, cover more ground, if we want a chance of finding them."

"We don't have enough counselors here to send out a big search party, you can only take a few. That's all we can afford," Venkman said.

"We'll do what we have to," I said, when my attention was brought to the screen door as it was slammed shut. It was Buzz with an adult male who wore a plaid shirt and orange vest.

"I believe this gentleman needs to speak with you

urgently," Buzz announced before excusing herself out of the door.

■ ■ ■

"We have to go back there together," I pled to Edgar. "We have to get him!"

Edgar picked up his brown wooden box and cradled it under his armpit. "You said it yourself, you saw him die when he fell into the gully."

"I don't know that! He could be hurt and he could have no way out of it. We need to help!"

He adjusted the box to fit comfortably against his body. "If we head back that way, we're never going to make it out of the forest before sundown."

"We can't just leave him!" I panicked.

Edgar sat on that for a second and stared at me.

"We could—we could go back to the rock quarry. There were people there, right? We could get help, have them use their radio, do a search party," I listed off. "Anything!"

"We have no clue where the water took his body," he replied.

I reluctantly let a tear drop down my face while I stared up at Edgar.

"Listen," Edgar said as he caught the desperation from me. "Listen—" He bent down on one knee so he was face-to-face with me. "We're pretty off course at this point, but if we start hiking, we can make it to the main road by dusk. If we catch a car coming our way, we can get help—we'll be able to bring back a whole army for your friend . . . " he left this open for me to fill in the blank.

"TJ," I said quietly as I looked down at the ground.

"TJ," Edgar repeated. "We're in just as much danger as TJ if we don't get moving. The sunlight is our friend. We don't want to leave it hanging."

Edgar trudged forward before realizing he could only hear his own footsteps. He turned around. "Well?"

I stood there and stared at him, conflicted by

the two roads of travel given to me. I looked over my shoulder to where TJ laid, possibly dead, if not worse— dying. In front of me I saw the road to safety, possibly help if not better—help for TJ. I made up my mind.

CHAPTER 9

THE SUN BEAT DOWN ON US AS WE HIKED FOR more than two hours without a break, save for a bathroom stop and a chance for me to collect a few stones I had recognized from my geology books.

"You really wanna tack on more weight to yourself while we do this? We still have a lot of distance to cover," Edgar asked.

I stopped and dropped the stones down at my feet, before I grabbed a seat on a tree stump. "You're right," I said, out of breath. "You think we can have a minute for a breather?"

Edgar stopped walking and turned back to me.

"Yeah, that's a good idea," he said and wiped his brow. He dropped the wooden crate to the ground, flipped it upright, and took a seat on it. "What kind of rocks did you find?"

I picked up a dark-colored rock the shape of a square and dangled it between my thumb and ring finger. "This is a basalt rock, I think," I said and dropped it back to the ground. I picked up another, lighter-colored rock. "This is shale. It's mostly a congealed mess of mud and minerals." I placed the shale piece directly on top of the basalt rock, then picked up another handful of rocks I had collected.

"Wow, how do you know so much about rocks?"

I placed a sandstone rock on top of the shale. "When you're not invited to many parties or have an iPad to drool over, you figure out quickly that the library is the closest thing you can get to a friend."

"I see," Edgar noted as his eyes followed my red, swollen hands.

"It's funny," I continued as I placed a chunk of limestone above the granite. "My whole life, I either felt like I didn't belong anywhere or people would just tell me straight up that I didn't." I watched the small tower of rocks tip to one side slightly, then hold still.

"It's like they think it's my brain that doesn't work, not my hands." I put a sandstone cherry on top of the stone sundae. "It's like giving myself the opportunity to grow and be someone I want to be—not remaining the helpless girl that people want to see me as." I looked up from my creation. "It's silly, I know. But that's what matters most. It's only up to me to change."

Edgar stayed silent, taking in my words.

"Can I ask you something?" I inquired while I picked at a scab on my elbow from the waterfall dive.

"Sure," Edgar finally answered.

"Can I see your ID?"

"My ID?"

"Yeah, your ID."

"Why do you want to see my ID?"

I didn't break eye contact. "The story. You were killed in the forest as a little boy."

Edgar let out a laugh to the sky.

"Everyone knows your name but here you are. Right in front of me. I need to know."

"You need to know, huh?" Edgar posed while he reached into his back pocket and tossed his brown leather J Crew wallet at my chest, watching as it tumbled to my lap.

"Well, as you can tell I didn't die in the forest," Edgar started. "I did go to Camp Dream Haven, that's true." Edgar looked up to the tree leaves and let the sunlight blind him momentarily. "I actually loved going there. The counselors were always so nice, especially about . . . " He pointed to his left eye with a twig.

I cracked one side of the wallet open to find his driver's license housed in a slot above a few credit cards. I slipped it out with the end of my thumb and evaluated the plastic ID. *Edgar Austin Hugo. DOB: 4-21-1976. Height: 5-10, Weight: 170.*

"But even the best times you have in your memory

get tarnished by something—or someone." He tossed the twig to the ground.

"What do you mean?" I asked, looking up from the picture of the man talking to me.

Edgar let out a sigh. "I know what you mean, when you said you either tell yourself that you're out of place or people make it their business to remind you of that."

"You do?"

"I get it more than you know." Edgar stood up. "I ran away from camp when the abuse became worse. It started off with name calling, then they started to destroy my things."

"You ran away? Like, into the woods?"

Edgar laughed. "By ran away, I mean I had my mom pick me up. I'm telling you, this 'legend' isn't terribly exciting."

"I'll say," I remarked with a smirk.

"It didn't take long to understand why they went after me—they had everyone in the camp to choose from, but I was the target."

"Just because of your glass eye?"

"Being a kid is hard enough as it is, you know? You want to be one of them—the normal ones. Adding a disability to it makes you see just how far you really are from everyone else."

Edgar walked around the crate. "My dad was already gone before I went to Dream Haven. Died of an infection in his gallbladder. So it was just me and mom. We had each other—we took care of each other. When she passed, I had nothing." He looked over at me. "And there's no better way to start over than to start with nothing."

"I'm sorry."

"It was hard at first. Well—it still is. I think about her every day. I did okay—went into finance banking, moved to the city, did everything everyone expected me to do as an adult. But like you said, I had to give myself the opportunity to grow and be someone I wanted to be—not remain the helpless person everyone saw me as."

"I said helpless *girl,*" I corrected him, which brought us both to a smile.

"Ah, I just needed something else, I needed to go somewhere where I could change. Somewhere that had defeated me before. A place I had to come back to and defeat, myself."

"This forest," I put it together.

Edgar smiled. "Nothing gives you a clearer idea of who you are better than the ability to conquer your own fears."

"Not to be offensive, but that sounds a little unhinged," I expressed. "I mean, you just left it all?"

"What's crazy about that when you've got nothing to leave behind? And it's not like I left it all behind. I still have my money and warehouse loft and sweet car. I just come out here when I need to get myself back on the rails."

I let the silence fill the space between us.

"I feel like I'm miles away from everyone else in my grade," I added. "It's like they have this secret club that I'm never going to be invited into." I looked down to the ground. "I think about that a lot."

"What?"

"What it's like to be normal."

"I don't think you and I are too far off."

"Really?"

"Sure, if there is something I've learned being out here, it's considering what normal is anyways." Edgar smiled. "And as far as I can tell, you and I fit the bill just fine."

I didn't respond in any way other than a smile.

Edgar bent down and picked up the crate again. "Well?"

I got up and rubbed my bloodied index finger on top of the stacked stones at my feet, which dried it off. "Let's go," I said and caught up to my guide.

CHAPTER 10

"Yeah, what is it that we can do for you?" Venkman asked.

"My named is Jarod. Jarod Taylor. You, uh—you guys have a few kids missing, is that right?"

I moved toward the man. "Yes! Yes! How did you know? Have you seen them?"

"Well, um—sort of . . . " Jarod replied.

"What do you mean, sort of?" Venkman interrogated.

"We're at the quarry, you know, down the Packer River. Well, this morning, we set the primer to go and just as the switch was flipped to blow . . . we saw two kids emerging from the forest."

"Flipped to blow . . . " I repeated and turned my attention to Venkman. "You knew. You knew they were blowing the quarry all along?!"

"I—I—" Venkman stumbled. "It's so far away from us that it never would have made a difference. You guys were on a one-day trip! You would have been nowhere near the blast." Venkman wiped sweat off of his forehead. "We needed to open and if we would have told them to hold off on the expansion, we would have never gotten the money . . . "

"You have no idea what you've just done," I said right in Venkman's face. I turned to the man in the orange vest, "Where are the kids?"

"They ran off back into the forest to avoid the explosion and water, we couldn't see where they went. After the blast, there was no way we could forge back in there to search. But I knew about this place, the camp, so I hightailed it here to tell you."

"You have a truck?" I asked.

"Sure do," Jarod responded.

"Jack, grab whatever tools you can gather. We're going back there."

"Well . . . " Jarod started. "There's something else . . . "

"What?" I asked.

"There is inventory missing from our site. Something we're worried about being gone, seeing that it can't just up and leave on its own."

"What was it?" Venkman questioned.

"A crate of dynamite," Jarod answered.

■ ■ ■

After another mile or so, I began to slow down, and my breath got heavier. I had to lean up against a tree.

"What? What's the matter?" Edgar asked, concerned.

I closed my eyes and breathed in and out heavily. After a few breaths, I opened my eyes and looked at Edgar.

"Nothing. It's just I haven't had my medication all day. I'm starting to get nauseated from the pain," I said, closed my eyes again, and winced.

"Is there anything I can do to help?"

I inhaled painfully, then opened my eyes back up. "No, I can do these hand exercises that can help for the time being," I said. I curved my fingers into an O and then flattened my hand straight again. "Unless you have any Trexall or Rituxan or even any olive oil since we're desperate enough . . . "

"Wait—olive oil?" Edgar asked curiously.

I continued to stretch my hands. "Hmm? Oh, yeah, olive oil helps with the inflammation of my joints if I rub some on them. Learned that one the hard way when I was on a road trip with my mom and brother. We were driving him to a basketball game out of state. I forgot my medication, my joints acted up when we were at some Italian restaurant for dinner. Fortunately, the doctor sitting next to us pointed out the olive oil dish for our bread would be helpful in this case. He was right."

"Well, I think I know a place nearby that just might have what we're looking for. Actually, it's a place I come to a lot out here, where I keep a reserve of camping stuff. And I'm pretty sure I have some olive oil left."

"It's close to here?" I asked hopefully.

"Yeah, just a mile or so over the ridge here. Do you think you can make it?"

"I don't think we have much of a choice," I said and pushed myself off of the tree. "Lead the way."

▪ ▪ ▪

"I can't let you do this, Telly," Venkman urged. "The media will be up here like a swarm of locusts once they catch wind of this."

I brushed past the camp director and threw a line of rope into the bed of Jarod's truck. "Yeah, well I don't think you have much say in the matter right now."

"Hey, I didn't put that map in your bag, okay? I'm trying my best here!" Venkman argued.

I grabbed a pack from Jack and without breaking my gaze with Venkman, I tossed it into the truck bed. "Your best? Your best is putting an entire camp of children in danger because of money?"

"There were issues I couldn't control. If I could have it both ways, then we wouldn't have had this problem. But I didn't, so as the camp director I had to choose." Venkman finished. "Those two going over that waterfall is certainly one that I could not steer for myself. What do you want me to do?"

I stopped loading up the truck and gazed straight through Venkman. "How about being a good person? My kid brother and another very innocent, very scared kid are out there alone trying to survive. And all you can think about is keeping this quiet."

Jack hopped into the bed of the truck after he threw the last of our things in there.

I climbed into the cab of the truck, next to Jarod, who was in the driver's seat. With one arm hung out of the window, I addressed Venkman for the last time. "Stay here until help arrives. And try not to push your irresponsibility onto anyone else while we're gone." And with that, I tapped the outside of the passenger door with my open hand and the truck took off down the gravel road.

I closed my eyes for a brief second and saw the bright white-and-orange tint from the sun behind my eyelids.

"I hope they're okay," Jarod's voice entered my train of thought.

I opened my eyes and looked straight at the exit of the camp. The sign above said, UNTIL NEXT TIME . . .

"It could be worse," I said, exhausted, and rested the side of my head on my fist.

We pulled the truck onto the paved road and picked up speed. The area was desolate, except for a wooden, waving Smokey the Bear next to a sign, which promoted: FIRE DANGER LOW TODAY! PREVENT WILDFIRES!

Jarod kept both eyes on the road. "What do you

mean? How does it get worse than having two missing kids traveling alone in a large, recently destroyed forest—possibly in possession of a large quantity of explosives?"

I let out a sigh. "It'd be worse if one of those two youths wasn't my brother."

"I don't follow exactly . . . " Jarod stated as he looked from the road to me for a second.

I pushed back on the truck bench, sitting tall with my shoulders squared. "TJ—TJ has always been rambunctious. Just like many other boys when they're growing up, they're just annoying as hell and all over the place. He was no different. He liked to kick up dust and see how far he could push things, and that brought along a reputation."

"What type of reputation?"

"Being a little punk, that type of reputation."

"Ah huh," Jarod followed.

"But it was understood that he wasn't malicious or out to try to hurt anyone. He actually made it a point to look after everybody he truly cared about. Almost in a deranged, obsessive way."

"Deranged?"

"TJ and our dad were close. Really close, and they did everything together. My dad was a fireman."

"Was?" Jarod asked.

I continued without answering him. "TJ would wait for him to come home from the station, and for the rest of the night they would not leave each other's side."

"Two years ago," I started before I could stop myself. "Two years ago, there was this grain elevator in our neighborhood. You know, one of those big concrete silos. It'd been there forever, since the thirties or whatever, and it had been closed down for decades. Kids would always find a way into it, though. It was illegal of course, but no matter what, the fire department was called just to be sure no one got hurt."

"One night, TJ blew up at my dad. It was a full-on meltdown, from what I remember. He never yelled like that, especially at Dad."

"What was it about?" Jarod asked, but kept his eyes on the road.

"Something stupid. I think my dad had plans to go out with friends, and TJ felt abandoned or betrayed. Like I said, stupid." I looked back out of the window. "TJ's response was to go missing and break into the grain elevator. After a few hours of being gone, someone in the neighborhood called it in. A kid. Possibly. On the roof of the grain elevator, overlooking the entire city."

"So the fire department was called, as usual. And of course my dad knew immediately who it was. So he called off the unit and went to get TJ himself. The silo was tall, probably one hundred and fifty feet high. And dad climbed up a rusted-out steel ladder, which was bolted into the concrete and took him straight to the top."

"He got TJ out safe, then?"

"Yeah, he got TJ out. He sent him down the ladder first. I guess my dad realized that the roof was going to give almost immediately, but didn't tell TJ. The panic would have made it more difficult."

"Made what more difficult?"

"The ladder wasn't going to hold both of them. He had no choice but to make sure that TJ was at the bottom and out of the silo before he started going down himself. But the roof collapsed, and took the ladder and my dad down with it."

Silence filled the cab of the truck, except for the hum of the engine and the crunch of gravel below the tires.

"I actually remember being sent home from school that day. Mom was in hysterics, talking to the police and my dad's fire unit. I found TJ upstairs. He was sitting in the middle of his room, covered in the dirt and grime from the collapsed silo. He didn't look at me or even acknowledge I was there. He just kept calling my dad's cell phone over and over. Expecting him to eventually pick it up. When he finally looked at me, I saw it right then and there in his eyes. He wasn't the same TJ anymore. That TJ was still in the silo.

Something switched off. He no doubt blames himself. So he's become destructive. Anti-social. You name it. He's completely washing away everything he was then so he never has to go through it again," Telly stopped and rethought that. "Well, almost everything."

"What do you mean?"

"Deep down, I know he can't get rid of who he is. It wasn't just taught to him, it's in his blood. So if he and Maddy are still together, he's going to keep her safe." I took a long, hesitant breath. "And if he's still alive, TJ's going to bring her home."

CHAPTER 11

THE WATER FLOWED QUICKLY BELOW ME, which made a soft trickling sound like snow melting off of the side of a rooftop. My left eye slowly opened while my right remained in the muddy bed of leaves and water. I coughed, making waves in the small pool of fresh water under my face. Goose bumps had risen on my bloodied, bare arms. I planted both fists below my chest and forced myself into a half push-up, but quickly collapsed back onto the ground.

"M-m-m . . . " I muttered and rolled onto my back.

I looked around from left to right, seeing only the

brown root- and rock-filled barriers on each side of the gully.

"M-m . . . " I choked out. "M-Maddy?"

I looked up above me and found a rootstock hanging out of the gully wall like a ladder rung. I grabbed onto it and tried to pull myself up to my feet.

"Maddy?!" I desperately screamed.

An immense pain shot from my thigh all the way through my body, which knocked me back down. I examined the dark crimson stain on the left pant leg of my jeans. A rock had passed completely through my thigh, missing my bone and anything else vital, *which is lucky*, I thought.

Outside of the leg wound and a splitting headache, everything else seemed to be in working order. I examined my body with my hands, double-checking that I didn't miss anything. Everything checked out until my fingertips landed on the sharp, jagged piece of stone sticking out of the right side of my forehead.

"What the . . . " I mumbled while I gingerly touched the rock lodged within my head. It wasn't far enough in to cause any real damage, I hoped. I ran through the ABC's in my head a few times just to make sure. I decided to leave the stone in, as it wasn't causing any trouble, as far as I could tell. Removing it was a job for a doctor.

But I needed to stop the bleeding from my leg—and quick. The river, which traveled around me and down the channel, was a swirl of brown and red, like the water used to clean up paintbrushes. I pulled myself up so I sat with my back against the wall of the gully. I undid my belt, wrapped it around my thigh above the wound, and pulled it to the very last hole in the line.

After the hard part was over, I grabbed a handful of mud from the ground next to me and smeared it directly over the wound. I went back for another fistful and did it on the underside of my thigh, and spread it smooth with my open hand.

The mud would cake up after it had dried, plug the hole, and help stop the bleeding. I knew there was a risk of infection that may come from doing that—but if I had to choose between bleeding out immediately or possibly getting a blood infection that would take a few days to set in, I'd choose the former all day and move on. There were more pressing matters at hand.

I was finally able to pull myself up to my feet and had to lean on the dirt wall to stabilize myself. I took a few practice steps that came with some minor pain from the pressure I put on the freshly dressed wound. I used the wall for support, and made my way down the gully and out into the open woods.

The uprooted tree we used as a shelter was still there; however, the raft was gone. I limped quickly to the shelter to see what I could find. In the hole, I found Maddy's backpack, tightly lodged between the tree and the ground. I bent slightly on one knee, tried not to disrupt the hardening mud, and wrenched it free. I held the bag in both hands and stared at the anime character brandishing its fist in my face as if threatening to pick a fight.

I was looking around for anything else when a

wad of gray and pink caught my attention out of the corner of my eye. I hobbled past the tree and picked up Maddy's zip-up hoodie. *This thing is comfortable in any temperature* I replayed in my head. I slipped the hoodie on one arm at a time and threw the backpack over my shoulder by one strap.

I evaluated my position and looked around. The water looked like it made its path of destruction heading west. If that were the case, then that certainly influenced what direction Maddy went. I had no choice in the matter anyway. The only option I had left in front of me was to go after her.

■ ■ ■

"Are we close?" I asked, losing steam.

"Yes, Maddy, hang in there. We're almost there," Edgar assured me.

The sun morphed from bright, magnificent yellow to a subdued orange and red. I stumbled along a few steps behind my guide, while my hands felt like they were dipped in gasoline and lit on fire. I questioned whether we'd get to our destination in time.

"We're here!" Edgar announced from just ahead while pointing downhill to an unseen location.

I made it up to Edgar and looked at the great sight below us. It was a large fortress made of plywood and ropes, and it looked like a castle from one of my renaissance architecture books. There were towers between the tall walls, an open courtyard in the middle, and a trench lined with sandbags that surrounded the building. Every inch of plywood was covered in splats of hot pink and neon green like pockmarks.

"What is this place?!" I asked in amazement.

"Welcome," Edgar said with his hand outstretched to the structure, "to the Bastion."

"The Bastion?"

"This used to be the town's old paintball fort that closed down many years ago. They'd drive us here when we were at camp to play paintball with other camps from around the area. It was to help create team building, I guess. I was never good at it due to poor aiming, but it was still a blast."

"This is amazing!" I announced.

"Well," Edgar offered, "shall we?"

"We shall!"

Edgar held onto my elbow, and we descended the hill together. We made it to the bottom to cross the drawbridge. As we approached the large unlocked door, Edgar pushed it with all of his might, so it swung wide open for us to enter. We entered the large open courtyard, and I turned around in astonishment and took in the great structure.

Despite being clearly fake and flimsy plywood, the details were incredible. There were bridges that connected towers with ropes and wood, doors that led to nowhere, and little walls in the middle of the courtyard for paintballers to take cover behind mid-battle.

"You keep your camping reserves here?" I asked after I examined it all. I noticed a burnt-out fire pit that looked recently used. "Like, you stay here?"

Edgar dropped his crate to his feet in front of the

fire pit. “Sure! It’s in the middle of nowhere; people have forgotten that it exists. It’s like my own personal castle.” Edgar explained. He started to set up an A-frame of wood within the fire pit. “I’ve conquered these woods, remember?” He thought for a second. “I guess that makes me the king!” he declared and struck a piece of flint into the wood, which made a small fire.

“Hah, yeah, I guess it does,” I agreed. The sun slowly went down behind the grand walls of the Bastion. I rubbed the knuckles of my left hand with the palm of my right, and Edgar noticed.

“Here, let’s get you set up. Follow me,” Edgar said, standing back up and leading the way across the big courtyard.

He opened a frail door that led into a dark chamber. Inside, there was a collection of stuff: canned food, water filters, rolled-up sleeping bags.

“Wow, you’re really prepared,” I observed. “You waiting for the world to end or something?”

Edgar laughed. "You never know what you're going to get into out here. Better safe than dead."

"I guess," I said while I fingered through the stuff strewn about while Edgar busied himself looking for the olive oil.

"Found it!" Edgar exclaimed and held up the short green bottle. "There isn't much left, will this do?"

"Yeah, I don't need much," I said as I took the bottle from him and poured what was left of it into my palm. I dipped my index finger into the pond of olive oil and started to rub it onto each individual joint on my hand. It began to soothe my pain enough to finally relax. I sat back with hands that glistened, and a look of relief across my face. "I needed that."

"Good," Edgar said with a smile.

"Okay, so, what do you think? Get back on the road now?"

Edgar turned his back to me and fiddled with things on the bench in front of him. "It's getting pretty dark, don't you think? We might have issues navigating through the forest to the road before dark."

"We need to go back for TJ," I insisted. "Here," I said and picked up a flashlight. I tried to flick it on, with no success. "We just need some batteries," I said and sifted through other stuff to find what I needed. Then I came across a kayak paddle and picked it up. "You have a kayak?"

"A kayak?" Edgar asked, confused, before recognition seeped into his voice. "Oh, yeah. I sure do. I make it a point to use it once a week up and down the Packer River. It's a great workout."

"Oh, interesting. I didn't notice any kayak while walking . . . " I said, turning the paddle over in my hand and revealing a name, A. Sheridan, painted on the handle in white. *A. Sheridan*, I repeated in my mind. Amanda Sheridan. The missing woman who was never found while canoeing down the Packer River. " . . . here," I finished.

Edgar didn't turn around. He just kept tooling with whatever it was in front of him on the bench. "Yeah, I keep it tied up on the river. That way I don't have to drag it back and forth."

I turned my attention to the dark corner of the chamber, where in the shadows lay tall, rusted black barrels. Two were hanging on the ceiling, connected to a pulley system attached to the wall. Like the type of barrels that were used to flip the raft on the river.

"I, uh—" I started, "I need to get some air. It's a little musty in here and my allergies are really starting to act up."

Edgar let out a long, disappointed sigh. "Put the paddle down," he said before closing the door to the chamber and twisting the lock. "I was hoping it wouldn't happen this fast."

■ ■ ■

I was panting heavily, but couldn't afford to stop. I had picked up a trail, possibly Maddy's from the size of the shoeprint. And someone else. Someone bigger than the both of us. And from the looks of it, they were leading the way.

I finally stopped when I saw a tower of rocks built

in front of a stump. *Slick move*, I thought to myself, examining the drying blood on the top stone. I wasn't far behind. The cairn told me that they were now heading north. Maddy wouldn't have left a message like this for me for no reason at all. She was leading me to them.

I knocked the cairn over, not needing anyone else to find it, before adjusting my direction and heading north.

▪ ▪ ▪

I swung the paddle at Edgar's head, but he easily blocked it, gaining control of the would-be weapon and throwing it to the ground. I ran around the wooden workbench, putting it between us.

"Come on, now," Edgar said, pulling a long knife out of the front of his brown hiking pants. "Just listen to me, okay?"

"You're a murderer!" I screamed across the bench, faking left and then moving right.

"I thought you and I were through with the name calling? That's not us! We need to stick," Edgar said, swinging the blade at me, "together!"

"I'm nothing like you!" I declared.

Edgar stopped and straightened himself up. "Oh, you and I are more alike than you could ever possibly know."

I remained still, both hands planted on the workbench between us, eyes fixated on Edgar. "That's impossible."

"Oh really?" Edgar asked, stabbing the knife into the workbench. "The only girl to show up to camp with zero friends. Hiding from your problems in the nurse's office. Immediately receiving and taking abuse from the popular jerk on campus." Edgar laughed. "I mean, come on. The clothes up the flagpole gag? What is this? The nineties?"

I focused my eyes on him. "How—how did you . . . " I saw it in his eyes. "You were watching us? At camp. You were watching us?"

"And what a show it was!" Edgar proclaimed with

both arms wide open. "I mean, I needed to scout out where I was going to plant the sticks of dynamite around the camp unseen."

My eyes widened. "You were going to blow us up!?"

"*Am*, yes," Edgar corrected. "But you, no. I'm afraid you won't be around for those fireworks."

"Why would you want to do that to a bunch of innocent people!?"

"Innocent? No chance," Edgar spat. "Each of them will grow up to be as toxic and venomous as they are now and live their lives like there aren't people who suffer every single day. But it's not the people that I'm interested in destroying. It is that . . . place. A house where children can be tormented and tortured for something they can't control. I'm stopping it from happening ever again. And it starts there." Edgar's eyes softened. "You of all people should get that. You of all people would gain the most from it happening."

I took that to heart. It was true; I would have been better off if there weren't people in my life who defined me by my hands. I shook my head clean of those thoughts. "No."

"No?"

"That's where you're wrong. I don't run away from or *blow up* my problems just because they make me feel bad. That's what makes up who you are and who you're going to be, by not letting it get to you," I said through my gritted teeth. "You're different because you couldn't handle it and you grew up with a chip on your shoulder big enough to make you into a psychopath. So, no," I said, looking over my shoulder at the pulley, "you and I are nothing alike." I waited to drop the bomb. "I'm not a giant pansy like you."

Edgar unleashed his fury over the bench, knife in hand. I stumbled backwards, making sure to grab the pulley system, which swung the two barrels directly into Edgar's chest, tossing his body through the flimsy locked door of the chamber.

I grabbed the green bottle of olive oil and leapt over Edgar's body. Dizzily, he grabbed my ankle, bringing me to the ground. I screamed while anchored to the dirt by the madman.

■ ■ ■

I heard a scream up ahead, so I hobbled to the edge of the hill overlooking a large wooden structure that loomed in the glow of moonlight. There was a small billow of smoke rising and a soft glow from the middle of the structure, undoubtedly from a bonfire. I found where her scream was coming from. I bent down, swinging the backpack to the front, and unzipped it. I dug through the bag and fished out what I was looking for—cherry lip balm.

■ ■ ■

I kicked Edgar once, then twice in the nose, wiggling my ankle free from his grasp. I rolled and stood up, stumbling backwards toward the bonfire, brandishing the bottle as a weapon. Edgar slowly rose, gaining his composure back. His nose looked like a snapped arrow.

"You broke my nose," Edgar said like he was stuffed up with a cold. He spit blood out of his mouth and motioned with his finger. "Come here."

I ran around the fire, knocking the crate of dynamite over. I threw the green bottle of olive oil into the fire pit, causing a big burst of flames to rise up. That didn't stop Edgar, who walked right through the blazing fire like a demon exiting hell. He grabbed ahold of me by my hands, squeezing hard and looking directly into my eyes.

"This could have been different. It could have been fast," he said, moving closer to my face. "But I'm going to make sure that I kill you as slowly. As. Possible."

I heard a whistle on the opposite side of the fire, causing both me and Edgar to look in its direction. We saw TJ quickly limp towards us and toss a handful of something through the flames of the fire. Before I could say anything, a dozen fireballs emerged from the flames, coming right at us. Most missed their target, hitting the wall of the Bastion and setting the place ablaze. One landed on Edgar's chest, lighting up his fleece zip-up, and another landed square on his right cheek, searing the flesh of his face. He ran off, screaming in agony.

One landed in my hair, starting it on fire.

■ ■ ■

"Ah, crap," I said running around the fire while stripping off the faded gray and pink hoodie and wrapping it around her head. "Hold still. Hold still!" I panicked, patting the fire out.

Maddy's voice came out muffled by the hoodie, "It's Edgar, Edgar Hugo!"

Before I knew it, a hulking mass took me down by the legs.

We rolled around briefly, but Edgar got the edge and was on top of me with both my arms pinned down under his legs. Edgar wrapped his hands around my throat and began to squeeze. He watched me struggle for air, letting his grip get tighter and tighter. I could feel my left eye begin to roll back into my head, while my face burned from the pressure.

Maddy was just a blur to me as she emerged from the smoky hoodie and saw the struggle happening between Edgar and me. She sprinted into the chamber, avoiding flames on both sides of her, grabbing some kind of wooden paddle.

I could feel my Adam's apple under Edgar's thumbs as he pushed in harder. Unable to squeeze any tighter, he screamed into my face, "I HATE YOU!"

I saw Maddy come up from behind, dragging the paddle in the dirt as she ran full speed at Edgar. Screaming through the pain, she raised the paddle high in the air and swung it down on Edgar's face, knocking a glass eye out of his skull. She stepped backwards.

Edgar turned to her, the empty eye socket gaping, and screamed. He leapt off me towards Maddy, taking her down to the ground. They tussled briefly, but

Maddy got on top, pushing the paddle into Edgar's neck. She was able to get her other hand planted on his face to separate the two of them.

I could hardly breathe, struggling to get air in and out of my throat. I looked behind me to see sticks of dynamite scattered out in front of a wooden crate. I used one leg and clawed my body towards them.

■ ■ ■

I struggled but was able to push the paddle harder onto Edgar's throat, who had my left hand between his teeth. He bit down, which released a stream of blood through his teeth.

"Ahhh!" I screamed in agony.

"Maddy!" TJ choked out.

I looked over and saw the twinkling stick in TJ's grasp. I released my grip on the paddle and jabbed my right index finger into Edgar's empty eye socket, fish hooking it to the side. He bellowed in pain, releasing his hold on my hand. I rose halfway up, then with all of my weight, dropped my knee into his groin, ending our struggle. Stepping on his face, I was able to get up and run.

TJ tossed the stick of dynamite into the mountain of rusted black barrels labeled PAINTBALLS behind Edgar's body. I made it to the other chamber, slamming the door behind me just in time.

■ ■ ■

As Maddy dashed away, I got my body behind a wooden wall in the middle of the burning courtyard. Edgar turned right when the stick exploded in front of him.

The thing about paintballs, at least what you don't usually hear, is that after thirty years of sitting dormant in rusty barrels in the hot summer heat, they become quite toxic. Polyethylene glycol is non-toxic by all means, but with that amount of time, anything can become extremely dangerous. So when Edgar became wrapped in steel shrapnel, steaming hot pink and bubbling neon green, you could see that the pain seared both inside and out.

Edgar's screams of misery receded into the night. From my view lying on the ground, I saw Maddy's shoes emerge from the blown-out chamber door. The entirety of the Bastion was up in flames now, and there was no escape in sight. Maddy ran to the toppled-over wall and found me under it. She looked at the heavy wooden obstacle and then to her hands.

"I'm out of spoons," she gravely stated. "Here, grab my legs!" She commanded, and I listened. I held onto her legs and pushed myself out while she walked backwards, pulling me from the wreckage. "We have to get out of here! Here," she said, wrapping my arm around her shoulders. "Come on!"

We made our way through the fiery maze, getting cut off by flames and collapsing architecture at every turn. There was no exit for us out of that inferno.

Maddy stopped and thought for a second. "TJ," she said. I looked up at her through the eye that wasn't swollen. "The escape fire. We need to make one."

The idea was, is, and always will be crazy. Yeah, I told that story about my grandpa a thousand times, but I also once told a story about how I accidently created Facebook for a school project. I don't know why, but we honestly had no other options if we wanted to survive that night.

I looked around and pointed at one of the used fire pits in the middle of the courtyard. "There!"

We both hobbled to the middle of the ashen pit, and I instructed Maddy to get on her knees. I got down on mine across from her.

"Put your face into the ground and surround yourself with the ash. Whatever you do," I directed, "don't look up and only breathe when absolutely necessary."

"Okay," Maddy complied before shoveling dirt toward her head with her open arms. We both laid there, faces in the dirt as the kingdom burned bright in the dark night's sky.

After a moment, I felt something nudging my

hand, causing me to look up. Maddy's hand had crossed the pit, wrapping mine in hers. I looked through the smoke into her eyes, which for some reason looked calm. Like this wasn't the worst it could possibly be. And it was true. Together, as we watched the world around us burn to the ground, at least in that very moment, we had each other.

CHAPTER 12

AND LIKE THAT, THE NIGHT TURNED TO DAY, and white smoke filled the bright morning sky. The deafening sound of blazing fire had turned to a muted crackle. All of the brilliant flames had softened into mere embers.

I was the first to look up. My bloodied, soot-covered face rose from the ashes and examined the scene. We were lying in the middle of a black forest. Everything but us had burned into nothingness.

TJ raised his head slowly, making sure the coast was clear. He found my gaze across from his, and even with my battered face and burned-up hair, I was the happiest I've ever been.

"Hey," he said. "I don't want to worry you, truly, but . . . "

"What?" I asked, suddenly distraught.

"You have a little something on your face," he joked. We both laughed.

"You got my message, then?" I asked, pointing at the burned skeleton of the Bastion.

"The handwriting in your rock stacking was a little messy, but I got the gist." TJ stood up and brushed the front of his jeans off. "I don't know if I would have made it out of this without you," he said bashfully.

"You can make it up to me by paying the library bill for the book you fed to the highway," I replied, picking myself up. I rummaged through debris and burnt wood and found what I was looking for. TJ's face twisted as I pulled the mildly toasted and absolutely filthy gray and pink zip-up hoodie on.

I raised my shoulders. "Like I said, it's comfortable . . . "

" . . . in any temperature. Yeah, I got it," TJ finished.

Our attention was brought to the slamming of a pickup truck door. It was Telly, the guy from the rock quarry, and Jack the counselor. Telly scanned the remains of the Bastion and then ran to her brother and me. She took both of us in with a hug one at a time.

"Why is it that wherever you go, you have to burn the place to the ground?" she asked TJ.

"I just wasn't feeling the vibe of the space. I needed to open it up a little," he smugly replied. "I'm guessing the smoke signal was tall enough for you to find us?"

"It was helpful, getting out here was a whole other ordeal." She looked around at the devastated plot of land before her. Sirens started to get closer, enveloping the area with their sound. One by one, cop cars, a fire truck, and then an ambulance showed up. "What the hell happened here!?"

TJ looked at me, at the burned-down Bastion, and then his sister. "We dealt with the explosion."

EPILOGUE

"Ahhh, what a bunch of bull crap!" the ten-year-old Benny Johnson declares, illuminated by the fire pit.

"What?" TJ asks, seated across the fire and now wearing a blue Dream Haven shirt of his own.

"You're telling me that you survived in the woods when being stalked by a killer, and all you had was a tube of lip balm and a rock sticking out of your head?"

"Yeah, so?" TJ defends himself.

There is a new batch of campers surrounding the

fire pit of Camp Dream Haven. The night is clear, with stars dancing around the full, shining moon.

"But you're supposed to be a liar. You make up stories all of the time," Benny points out.

"I wouldn't have believed it either if I weren't there myself," Maddy, also wearing a Dream Haven shirt, chimes in, taking a seat next to TJ. "But this is how it happened," she assures.

"I second that," Telly adds while dropping off an armful of firewood in front of the pit. "Although, there was a lot more dramatization in this telling than the last time you told this story."

"I was adding theatrics to make it more accessible to a wider audience," TJ professes, looking at the new campers.

"So you made it up!" Benny shouts.

"Okay—fine, here," TJ says while moving some grown-out hair away from his forehead. "You see this freaking crater in my head?"

Benny and the rest of the campers recoil. "Do you like that one?" TJ taunts while pointing at the indented scar left in his forehead by the rock quarry debris. "How about this?" he asks while lifting the leg of his shorts to reveal a similar scar deep within his thigh.

"Ewww," the campers squeal in unison.

"Don't forget this one," Maddy adds while pulling back the sleeve of her patched-up gray and pink hoodie, revealing a perfect set of maroon teeth marks left on the side of her hand.

"Whooaaa," the chorus of campers sings.

"But that wasn't the point of the story," Maddy laughs. "We're stuck with these scars for the rest of our lives, and that's not a bad thing." She pulls her sleeve forward. "We use them as a reminder to not go back to that dark place that brought us to the woods."

"Something Edgar could never do," TJ adds.

"So what's the point of the story, then?" Benny asks.

"The point of the story is that being thrown into the middle of the woods isn't the worst thing you have to survive," Maddy articulates. "Childhood is the hard part. You either learn to survive it, or you let it get the best of you and never come back."

"If there is something we did pick up because of this," TJ interjects, looking at Maddy, "it's that it makes it a lot easier if you have a helping hand."